*"It was uncomplicated and great—at least, that's what you told me at the time. But now you're using that fact to make me sound like some sort of tramp!"*

Steeling himself against the venom spitting from Catrin's eyes, Murat shook his head. "My intention has never been to make you feel bad about yourself, but I never promised you marriage, Cat. I made that clear from the start. And yes, I always said I would be honest with you. I told you that I had very particular specifications for my bride. That I required a woman of royal blood who would behave as a future desert queen would be expected to behave. And I'm afraid that you were..." His voice trailed away, but once again, she didn't seem prepared to let it go.

"I was what, Murat?"

He sighed, wondering why women always did this. Even Cat. Why they always provoked you to a certain point and made you say something that afterward you would both regret. He shook his head. "It doesn't matter."

"Oh, but it does. It matters very much."

He shrugged. "I'm afraid you were neither."

**Desert Men of Qurhah**

*Their destiny is the desert!*

The heat of the desert is nothing compared to the passion that burns between the pages of this stunning new trilogy by Sharon Kendrick!

### *Defiant in the Desert*

December 2013

Oil baron Suleiman Abd Al-Aziz has been sent to retrieve the sultan of Qurhah's reluctant fiancée—a woman who's utterly forbidden, but is determined to escape the confines of her engagement...by seducing him!

### *Shamed in the Sands*

February 2014

The princess of Qurhah has always wanted something different from her life. So when sexy advertising magnate Gabe Steele arrives to work for her brother, Leila convinces Gabe to give her a job...but that's not the only thing to cause a royal scandal!

### *Seduced by the Sultan*

April 2014

The sultan of Qurhah is facing a scandal of epic proportions. His fiancée has run off, leaving him with a space in his king-size bed. A space once occupied by his mistress—Catrin Thomas. And now he wants her back—at any price!

# Sharon Kendrick

—

## Seduced by the Sultan

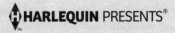

HARLEQUIN PRESENTS®

Recycling programs
for this product may
not exist in your area.

ISBN-13: 978-0-373-13232-4

SEDUCED BY THE SULTAN

First North American Publication 2014

Copyright © 2014 by Sharon Kendrick

**Printed in U.S.A.**

www.Harlequin.com

**All about the author...**
*Sharon Kendrick*

**SHARON KENDRICK** started storytelling at the age of eleven and has never really stopped. She likes to write fast-paced, feel-good romances with heroes who are so sexy they'll make your toes curl!

Born in west London, she now lives in the beautiful city of Winchester—where she can see the cathedral from her window (but only if she stands on tip-toe). She has two children, Celia and Patrick, and her passions include music, books, cooking and eating—and drifting off into wonderful daydreams while she works out new plots!

Visit Sharon at www.sharonkendrick.com.

**Other titles by Sharon Kendrick available in ebook:**

SHAMED IN THE SANDS *(Desert Men of Qurhah)*
DEFIANT IN THE DESERT *(Desert Men of Qurhah)*
THE GREEK'S MARRIAGE BARGAIN
A WHISPER OF DISGRACE *(Sicily's Corretti Dynasty)*

To ace surgeon Mike Heard for his invaluable help with research—and to his lovely legal-eagle wife, Janie, for all the help she's going to give me in future (I hope!)

# CHAPTER ONE

*'YOU'RE NOTHING BUT a rich man's whore!'*

The words still burned in Catrin's ears and she couldn't seem to shift them, no matter how hard she tried. Hateful words made worse by the fact that they had been spoken by her own mother.

*'What the hell do you think he's doing when he's out of the country?'* Ursula Thomas had demanded. *'Going to bed early, with nothing but a book in his hand?'*

Catrin had sat listening to the slurred words, feeling all her confidence drain away. But she couldn't deny that the accusations had touched a raw nerve and that was probably why she had reacted so defensively. Why her nails had dug into the palms of her hands so hard that it hurt and instead of telling her mother it was none of her business, she had stupidly tried to justify herself. Because that was pointless. Some people only ever saw the dark side of life and her mother was one of them.

She was *not* a whore.

And Murat *was* going to bed on his own.

Catrin let her thoughts stray to the exotic Sultan who had changed her world. She had never planned to be a 'kept woman' living in a fancy penthouse, but that was the way things had turned out. Just as she had never planned a relationship with a man who was larger than life—a man for whom the rules *had* to be broken. Only now she had broken the most dangerous rule of all and she didn't know what she was going to do about it.

Later, he would arrive here from Qurhah. He would take her in his arms and the undiluted pleasure of his kiss would quickly block out everything else. But she wondered for how long. How long before the niggling doubts returned—along with the growing certainty that she had done what she had vowed never to do?

She had fallen in love with him.

She *loved* Murat.

It was the worst of all possible scenarios.

She walked over to the window and stared out. How had that happened? Especially to someone who didn't 'do' love? Who had always claimed—with good reason—that she didn't know what love was. She wondered when that invisible switch had been flicked. The one which had changed everything and made her heart race whenever she thought of him. Was it logical to love a man who was never really there for her, who had never offered her anything but fabulous sex and pretty baubles?

But love wasn't logical, was it? It crept up on you whether you wanted it to or not. And that was dangerous. More to the point, it was futile. Because the only thing the Sultan had ever promised her was that he could never commit.

Her gaze moved to the distant treetops and the green canopy of leaves which were moving gently in the soft summer breeze. Sometimes it was hard to believe that this apartment was slap-bang in the centre of London—with a view dominated by a park so beautiful that sometimes it felt just like being in the countryside. Just as it was hard to believe that the sleek woman who stared back at her from the mirror every morning really *was* Catrin Thomas, the small-town woman who had given herself so completely to the autocratic desert King of Qurhah.

Gone was the unruly tangle of shiny curls which had once defined her and in their place were waves of hair so glossy that someone in a shop had once stopped her and told her she should be in a shampoo commercial. Gone were the cheap clothes she used to buy on her very average salary and the cut-price make-up she used to pick up from the nearby super-market. These days she looked expensive because she *was* expensive. A rich man's mistress. With a price tag to match.

The telephone began to ring and Catrin rushed to answer it as soon as she saw Murat's name flash up on the screen, because he hated to be kept waiting. But she accepted that, as she had accepted so much else about him. He was a sultan and a king. He ruled a vast and affluent desert region. He wasn't *used* to waiting. His time—as she knew only too well—was very precious.

'Hello?' she said, breathlessly, because a phone call meant that his private jet was already in the air and soon he would be landing at the small airfield just outside London. *And she was nowhere near ready!*

'Cat? Is that you?'

She sucked in an excited breath, because his deep, accented voice always had the same effect on her. It made her stomach twist into knots. It made her skin prickle with anticipation. Only now, of course, it also made her heart lurch with anxiety—because this was not just the 'friends with benefits' thing any more. This was—most inconveniently—that stupid thing called love and she must be careful not to show it.

'Of course it's me,' she said softly. 'Who else could it be?'

'It didn't sound like you.' There was a pause. 'For a minute I thought you might have gone away and left me.'

His voice had dipped in that indulgent way it always did when they hadn't seen each other in a while. A whole month had passed since Murat had last been in England. It had been the longest time they'd ever been apart, and Catrin had missed him. She'd missed him like crazy.

'I think we both know,' she said, trying not to let her voice tremble with emotion, 'that I'm not planning on going anywhere.'

'I'm very pleased to hear it.'

But something in his voice caused her to grow still, as a flicker of foreboding iced its way over her skin. She frowned. 'You sound a little…weary, Murat.'

'I am—or rather, I was. But suddenly I discover that I am filled with energy at the thought of seeing you again, my beautiful, green-eyed little Cat.'

She could hear the sudden roughening of his voice and wished that he were here now and that he were kissing her. Kissing her and making all these stupid doubts disappear into thin air. 'Me, too,' she said.

'And I'm wondering,' he murmured, 'what you've been doing to make you sound so breathless?'

The words were on the tip of her tongue, but she didn't say them, even though part of her wondered what his reaction would be if she came out with the truth. *Oh, you know. I was just getting over the shock of hearing my mother tell me that I'm nothing but a whore and implying that you're up to no good when you're not here.*

But she had vowed to herself a long time ago that there was no point in objecting to things which couldn't be changed. She was trying to live in the moment. To enjoy what she had, instead of obsessing about what she didn't have, and could never have. Hadn't her own childhood taught her that was the *only* way to live?

'Not a lot,' she prevaricated. 'I was just wondering what time you're going to get here.'

'Soon, my beauty. Very soon. But I don't want to waste time talking about my schedule when there are so many more interesting things we could discuss. And there's only one thought on my mind right now after so many weeks of being away.' There was a pause. 'What are you wearing?'

Catrin's perfectly manicured nails tightened around the handset of the phone and she swallowed down the sudden lump which had risen in her throat. She knew what was expected of her and usually it was all too easy to play this game. Of course it was—because Murat had taught her the rules and, consequently, she had become very accomplished at it. And she *liked* it. She liked playing the sexy mistress who was up for it any time of the day or night.

But today the seeds of uncertainty had been sown in her mind. She felt like a tennis player who had walked out on court to find an enormous hole at the centre of her racquet.

*So pull yourself together,* she urged herself. *Count your blessings and enjoy the life you've been given instead of the one you secretly crave.*

She ran her hand over one hip, her fingertips encountering the rough texture of her denim jeans. But instead of describing an article of clothing which Murat despised, she injected a sultry note into her voice and pretended. Because wasn't fantasy everything to lovers? Hadn't he taught her *that*, too?

'I'm wearing silk,' she whispered.

'What kind of silk?'

That stupid lump was still sticking in her throat, but it didn't stop her from continuing with the game. Quite honestly, she couldn't imagine having a telephone conversation with Murat which *wasn't* erotic. The kind of conversation she'd never have been able to carry off when she'd just been that naïve girl from Wales. But in spite of her background, she'd always been smart. She devoured books and was a fast learner—and learning to please a man was a skill just like any other, just like arranging flowers or making a cake rise.

'Soft silk,' she said. 'Butter soft.'

'Tell me more.'

She thought about the ribboned and crotchless purchase still lying in folds of soft tissue paper in the bedroom. The one she was planning to slide into as soon as she'd had her shower. The one which would probably be ripped apart by Murat's impatient fingers within minutes of his arriving here. 'They're midnight blue,' she said, almost conversationally.

'Excellent.' A pause. 'And are they tiny panties?'

'Oh, yes. So tiny you can barely see them. Honestly, it's almost a waste of time me wearing them—they're so flimsy.'

'I see.' Another pause—much longer this time. 'And you have on a matching bra, I hope?'

'Oh, yes.' She paused—trying to rid herself of the sudden feeling of guilt which settled on her skin like a cold mist. Telling herself that she had nothing to be guilty about. That Murat liked these games. *And so did she.*

And that her mother's words meant nothing. *Nothing.*

'The bra is a bit on the small side,' she continued,

allowing her voice to dip into a provocative note as her imagination took wings. 'But it's edged with lace, so at least my nipples aren't *completely* on show.'

He didn't answer. At least, not straight away.

'And stockings?' His eventual response was unsteady; his tone gratifyingly deep. She heard him swallow and that was gratifying too. 'Are you wearing stockings?'

'Mmm,' she agreed, closing her eyes to blot out the sight of her jeans. 'Of course I am. Black silk stockings all the way from France. Though they cling to my thighs terribly in this heat.'

'I'd like to see them do that,' came his husky response. 'And then I'd like to peel them off, very slowly.'

'Would you?'

'Mmm. And then I'd like to slide my tongue up between your thighs and lick you until you come. Would you like that, my beauty?'

But for some stupid reason the fantasy suddenly evaporated, like champagne which had been left in a glass too long. Catrin's eyes snapped open and in one instant, she felt completely flat. 'Of course I would. I'd like it very much. What time...what time will you be getting here?'

'Soon,' he repeated. 'Very soon.'

Catrin was just about to say goodbye and hang up, when she heard the sound of a key being inserted into a lock and her head jerked up in surprise. She turned towards the sound and nearly dropped the phone when she saw who was standing there.

Her first thought was that it couldn't possibly be Murat because his timetable was always planned to the nearest second—and her next thought was that it couldn't be anyone else. Because there was no one in the world who could be mistaken for him. No man matched him, nor ever could.

Murat the Mighty, they called him in his country of Qurhah, but he was also known as Murat the Magnificent—and he looked nothing less than magnificent now.

His hair fell in rich, dark waves around the hard outlines of his face and the soft sensuality of his lips contrasted with the distinctive hawk-like nose and ebony glitter of his eyes. He had the body of a desert warrior—a fact which could never quite be disguised by the Italian suits he favoured when in the west. Catrin knew that back home in Qurhah he wore flowing robes and headdresses but she'd only ever seen him in this kind of clothes, except in photos. And sometimes when she looked at those photos, didn't it make her wistful that she only ever got a tiny part of him? That so much of his life was forbidden to her.

'Murat?' she said, her voice rising in surprise. 'I wasn't expecting you yet.'

'So I see,' he replied, shutting the door softly behind him. He began to walk towards her, a complicit smile lifting the corners of his lips as he cut the connection on his phone and slid it into the pocket of his trousers. But his gaze was thoughtful as he looked at her, as if her response wasn't what he had been expecting. 'Aren't you going to say hello to me... properly, my beauty?'

'Hello,' she said, putting down her own phone with fingers which had started to tremble.

There was a pause as Murat let his gaze travel over her body, his eyes narrowing. Something about her was different and at first he couldn't work out what it was. Something which made his heart twist in a way which was unfamiliar. And then he realised what it was. She looked like the Cat he'd first met. The beautiful, country girl who had captivated him from the moment she'd turned those extraordinary green eyes in his direction and blinked at him, as if she couldn't quite believe what she had seen.

Dressed down and casual, her hair was dishevelled—almost wild. The dark cascade of waves tumbled down around her shoulders as if she'd been frantically running her fingers through it. And her *clothes*...

Her glorious legs were covered with jeans—a garment he despised on women and which she had tacitly agreed never to wear in his presence. And although her thin T-shirt outlined her breasts in a way which couldn't fail to please him—this wasn't what he had been anticipating.

He thought how much she had changed. How his rough diamond had become a smooth and polished gem. And if sometimes he missed the rather outspoken minx he had first seduced, he could not deny that she had grown into her role well. Almost too well...

'You promised me stockings,' he said slowly.

Her fingers flew to her hair, as if she had suddenly become aware of its unruliness, and she stared down at her jeans before looking up at him, a faint look of guilt staining her face.

'I didn't realise you were so close,' she protested.

'I thought I'd surprise you.'

'You've certainly done that.'

Their eyes clashed. 'So. No welcoming kiss for your sultan?' He shrugged off his jacket and draped it over the back of a chair. 'Not even a hug?'

She chewed on her lip as if she wanted to say something but didn't dare and for a moment Murat felt an unexpected twinge of conscience. Maybe it had been unfair of him not to warn her that he was on his way from the airport and that he had brought his schedule forward by several hours. But he had wanted to see her and he knew that there wouldn't be many more opportunities like this.

Because lately he had become increasingly aware that the clock was ticking on this relationship of theirs, and that some time soon he must sit down and talk to her seriously about the future. There were things he needed to tell about his life. Things she ought to know.

But not today.

His mouth flattened.

It was never today.

*Today he just intended to make the most of these moments, which had never been intended to last.*

His mouth softened into a smile and that was when a breath seemed to catch in her throat before she flashed him an answering smile. Running across the room, she hurled herself into his arms with all the eagerness of a puppy, coiling her hands around his neck as she clung to him. He could feel the softness of her breasts as she pressed herself closer. And he could feel the sweet warmth of her breath as she showered tiny kisses all over his face.

'Oh, Murat,' she said, shakily. 'I'm sorry. Hello again. Hello properly this time.'

Her mouth moved towards his and Murat groaned as their lips met. She kissed more sweetly than any other woman he'd ever known. But then, she made love more sweetly than any other woman he'd ever known. Was that because he had moulded her to become his perfect lover? Because he had coached this naïve little beauty to become as skilful as any practised courtesan, or woman of the harem?

Her lips were opening wider and she was darting the tip of her tongue against his as if she wanted nothing more than to taste him. The tips of her nipples felt hard against his chest and suddenly Murat forgot that he'd been promised stockings. Forgot that he liked his mistresses to be permanently pampered and prepared for him. Because this was Cat. Captivating Cat who made him feel weak with desire. Who exerted over him a power which no other woman had come even close to.

'Cat.' The word came out like a husky plea. 'I have missed you. By all the flowers that bloom on the Mekathasinian Sands, I have missed you.'

She pulled away from him then, her eyes searching his face with a curious kind of intensity. 'Have you?'

'You really need to ask a question like that?'

She nodded in response, but not before he had seen a sudden cloud pass over her features.

'Yes, Murat. I do. Sometimes…' Her voice faltered. 'Sometimes a woman needs to hear these things.'

'Then let me tell you all the things you need to hear, and more. I have missed you very much.' He buried his lips in the thick lustre of her hair. 'I have ached for you. Each time I galloped across the desert sands, I thought of nothing but you. During those long and sometimes tedious meetings of state affairs, I longed for one glance from those green eyes and to feel the silk of your skin, gliding beneath mine. I wanted to lie on top of you. I wanted to be inside you. To plunge into your molten heat and lose myself deep in your body. So come with me, my dark-haired beauty. Let me take you to bed, before I go out of my mind with frustration.'

Catrin stared into black eyes which had grown smoky with desire, but the same doubts which had been niggling away at her all week were refusing to go away. He was turning her on the way he always did, but a small voice in her head was asking whether he might not want to *talk* to her first. It had been weeks since they'd seen one another and something about his attitude was making her feel like an object on which he clearly wanted to slake his lust. Surely for once he could go through the motions of actually wanting to do something other than instantly have sex with her.

*You're nothing but a rich man's whore.*

She swallowed as her mother's drunken words came echoing back. What would Murat say if she offered him coffee first—or coolly told him she needed to take a shower after rushing back from Wales this morning?

But somehow her body wasn't listening to these silent objections—it was listening instead to the fierce sexual hunger which Murat had liberated. So she hesitated for no more than a second before letting him lead her towards the master bedroom, as helplessly as a moth to the flame.

Her doubts began to dissolve as he peeled the T-shirt over her head and dropped it to the ground. And soon all her uncertainties were vanquished by the simple action of the mighty Sultan tugging at her jeans and saying something in his native tongue before pushing her down onto the bed.

She was wearing the more practical underwear she tended to opt for when Murat wasn't in town, because the thongs he favoured tended to ride up between the crack in her bottom and weren't terribly practical when she was running around. Today she had on plain white panties without a frivolous element in sight.

He stared down at the sensible piece of lingerie for a long moment before reaching down to touch it, his hand brushing over her searing heat before moving aside the moist white panel to gain more intimate entry. He prised apart her molten flesh and she writhed a little as he pleasured her, before he withdrew one glossy finger and started licking it— with a slow eroticism which set her senses sizzling.

'Oh,' she said, her disappointment evident as he moved away from the bed.

'Be patient, my little pussy Cat. And let me lose this damned suit.'

Catrin squirmed with anticipation as she watched him undressing, revealing the magnificent body beneath. The olive-skinned perfection of his torso was marred only by a scar which arrowed across one side of his abdomen. When she had first seen it, she had run wondering fingers along the raised ridge and asked him whether he had sustained a wound in battle. And he had responded rather drily that it was the legacy of a childhood appendectomy, performed at the children's hospital in Qurhah's capital city of Simdahab.

The rest of his clothes were quickly discarded and she saw just how aroused he was—his erection completely dominating her line of vision as he joined her on the bed. She could feel its hardness pushing against her belly as he leaned over her and ripped open her brassiere with a hunger he didn't bother to hide.

She told herself she should be despairing that yet another costly piece of lingerie would now be unwearable—but right then she didn't care. She didn't care about anything except feeling him inside her again.

What did he do that made her feel like this?

*What did he do that made her love him so?*

'Murat,' she moaned, brushing her mouth over his jaw and feeling its rough graze beneath her lips. 'Oh. Murat.'

'What is it, my sweet?' His deep voice shuddered with undisguised pleasure. 'Tell me.'

She wondered what he would say if she told him the truth. If she told him she wished he would confound the gloomy expectations of her mother and make a decent woman of her. She wondered how he'd react if he knew that night after lonely night, when he was back in Qurhah and she was lying alone in this great big bed—sometimes she allowed herself to fantasise about marrying him. About him taking her back to his desert country as his bride...his *Sultana*—where she would learn to speak his language and bear him fine, strong sons and live with him to the end of her days.

She guessed that he would probably recoil with horror—and then she wouldn't see him for dust. Because after more than a year of her being Murat's mistress, any sign of commitment was just as distant as it had been when he'd plucked her from the valleys and brought her to London, quivering with passion and innocence and a fierce sexual hunger.

He'd said from the start that there was no future in this relationship and that marriage was never going to happen. She'd known that when he took a bride, it would be one as unlike her as it was possible to be. And even though she'd told herself she was fine with that, sometimes she wondered if she was just kidding herself. Lately, she had found herself longing for some kind of commitment. For the comfort and security she'd never really had.

But that was a waste of time *and* energy.

'Would you like me to tell you how much I missed you?' she said eagerly.

'You may tell me whatever you please, my beauty—just as long as you let me reacquaint myself with these magnificent breasts of yours,' he said, disposing of the now tattered brassiere with a careless flick of his fingers. 'For I have been dreaming about licking them like this.'

Catrin stifled a moan. 'So have I.'

'Shall I play with your pretty nipples?' he continued. 'Shall I lick them and suck them and make you wet in lots of different places?'

'Oh, yes, please,' she breathed.

'And is there anything else I should do?' His hand began to move down over the concave dip of her torso. She felt the exploratory caress of his palm as it skated over her belly, a forefinger briefly circling the faint dip of her navel before it continued its journey. 'Anything else I can tempt you with?'

'Can't you…guess?' she whispered.

'I can try. I think you might want me to slide down these rather schoolmistressy panties you're wearing…'

'You don't like them?'

'They are a fantasy I didn't realise I had until now. I just want to get the damned things off.'

His finger hooked inside the garment to give action to his words, but then it stilled. Lifting her head to see why, Catrin looked into his face and she saw something in his eyes she didn't recognise. Something which made her screw her face up in confusion because…was it *sadness* she read there?

'What is it?' she whispered. 'Murat—is something *wrong*?'

But the sadness—if that was what it had been—had now been replaced by the much more familiar smoulder of lust.

'No, nothing is wrong,' he growled as he slid the panties down over her knees and started to kiss her.

Catrin shuddered out a sigh as he brought her closer to him, because this was a dance she knew so well that it had become almost second nature to her. Her sexual experience before she'd met Murat had been zero, but the Sultan had changed all that. He had taught her so much. To trust her body and to love it. And that sex was the most sublime of all pleasures and she should never feel guilty about enjoying it.

A whole month of being without him had left her feeling desperate to touch him like this. She marvelled at the seamless slotting of their bodies. She cried out with joy as he entered her.

'Oh, Cat,' he murmured as he paused to allow her body to accommodate him.

'You feel so…good.'

'And so do you,' came his unsteady response. 'Sweet storm of the desert—so do you!'

Murat felt his mouth grow dry as he concentrated on each exquisite thrust. His hands cupped the silken globes of her buttocks as he moved deeper inside her. He thought that she felt like velvet. Hot, smooth velvet. He wanted this feeling to last. He wanted to stay trapped inside her and to spend the rest of the night kissing her soft, sweet lips. But nothing lasted. He knew that. And the sudden bitterness of what lay ahead made him drive into her more deeply still.

Her body began to arch and to quiver as the first spasm of orgasm claimed her and he took just long enough to watch the flush which bloomed over her breasts, before he too went under. Crying out in his native tongue, his seed seeming to burst from him in a fierce explosion of pleasure.

Time slowed and a torpor began to steal over him. He lifted a lazy hand to tangle his fingers in her hair but he could see a sudden wariness on her face as she gazed at him. He wanted to sleep but it seemed she was not keen to let him.

'So what brought you back so early?' she questioned, leaning over him so that her long hair tickled his chest.

'I juggled my schedule a little.' He yawned. 'There's someone I need to see. In fact, we're having dinner with him tonight.'

'But—' she frowned '—I've made gazpacho—and some lemon soufflé.'

He laughed. 'Now you sound like a housewife.'

There was a pause. 'I thought you liked me to play housewife.'

'Well, sometimes I do.' *And sometimes I don't.*

'And you always reserve your first evening back for just the two of us.'

'I know I do.' He failed to stifle a second yawn. 'And I'm sorry, Cat—but this meeting can't be postponed.'

'Right.'

Murat registered the disappointment in her voice even though she was doing her best to disguise it. Yet surely she must realise that she had been given more access to him than any other woman he'd ever known. Maybe now might be a good time to remind her. But the sudden darkness which was clouding her eyes made him want to placate her instead, so he stroked his hand down over her hip. 'But you will enjoy meeting Niccolo. He's flying to New York in the morning and so it made sense to meet him here in London.'

Her face relaxed a little. 'Not the infamous Niccolo Da Conti who I've never been allowed to meet before? One of your *Three Musketeer* friends?'

'Yes, that's him,' said Murat. 'And it's not a case of you not being allowed to meet him—it's just that our paths don't often cross in London, which is why I usually meet up with him in Qurhah.'

'And I'm never allowed to set foot in Qurhah, am I?'

'Unfortunately, no.' With a soft growl he extended his hand and pulled her closer and as soon as he felt the softness of her body, he wanted her again. 'But I don't want to talk about all the factors which keep us apart. In fact, I don't want to talk about anything.

I haven't seen you for almost a month and there's only one thing on my mind. So lean over and kiss me, Cat.'

She did, of course. Because how could any woman resist a man as gorgeous as Murat the Magnificent? Against the whiteness of the bedding, his body gleamed like burnished gold. He was like a god, she thought as she lowered her head to brush her lips over his. A dark golden god, lying next to her.

But, out of nowhere, that scary feeling came back again. The one which made her feel as if she were falling off the edge of a cliff in slow motion. The one which gave her more pain than pleasure. The one which made her silently want to scream her denial. She *wasn't* in love with him. She didn't want to be. There was nothing to be gained from loving him.

More of her mother's words came filtering back and she didn't seem able to silence them.

*Has he spoken to you about the future, Catrin? Has he?*

Catrin moved restlessly. No, he most certainly had not. Their relationship contained plenty of fancy bows—but no strings. The future had been discussed and dismissed at the very beginning. Put away in a drawer which had been slammed shut and locked away.

'Stop frowning like that,' he murmured. 'And feel this instead.'

His boast was unashamedly sexual as he guided her hand between his legs and her cheeks grew hot as she met the mocking look in his eyes. Her fingers curled around his silken hardness as he pulled her mouth down towards his, and suddenly there was nothing in her mind but sensation.

She wondered if she was a weak person, because all her doubts flew straight out of her mind as soon as Murat began to kiss her. Yet this, more than anything else, felt right and, oh, so familiar.

Her thoughts splintered as she felt his fingers begin to explore her flesh, because hadn't it always been this way? Hadn't the chemistry between them exploded from the moment their paths had first crossed, when the impossible had happened?

And a humble girl from the valleys had captured the eye of a powerful and impossibly wealthy sultan.

# CHAPTER TWO

IT HAD BEEN one of those amazing mornings in Wales, where spring came later than anywhere else in Britain. Blossom was frothing like candyfloss on the trees, and all you could hear was birdsong. Nobody could have predicted that the peace of the small town was about to be broken by the arrival of an exotic stranger with his convoy of bodyguards, who all carried guns beneath the straining suits which covered their bulky frames.

Catrin had been enjoying life and relishing her freedom. She'd finally escaped from the poisonous atmosphere of home and found herself a job in a small hotel on the other side of Wales, though she was still close enough to pay duty calls to her mother. Their relationship had always been difficult, and if it hadn't been for her younger sister, then Catrin would have left home much sooner. But you couldn't leave a young girl alone to live with a drunk, could you? Just like you couldn't stop someone from hitting the vodka, no matter how many bottles of the stuff you tipped down the sink.

Her whole life felt as if it had been consumed with shielding her sister from the daily drama of their mother's life, but with Rachel now at university Catrin had been able to make a new life for herself.

Freedom felt heady. It made her feel giddy—like a new-born lamb stumbling from the darkness into a sunlit meadow. No longer did she feel fearful whenever she opened the door. She didn't have to rescue anyone or bail them out. She didn't have to pretend that things were hunky-dory when patently they were not. She could stay out late and not have to explain herself. Not that there were many opportunities to stay out late—when the nearest big town was miles away and the buses irregular. It was just the principle of freedom which she found so exhilarating.

She was trained for nothing in particular, but she was bright and adaptable and her willingness to work meant that the rest of the hotel staff liked her. Her bookworm habit had given her a knowledge of the world which didn't match her haphazard schooling, which meant she could talk easily to anyone—so the customers liked her, too. A year after joining the Hindmarsh Hotel, she could begin to see a future for herself in the hospitality industry.

The barmaid had been off sick one day and Catrin had stepped in at short notice, when Murat Al Maisan walked into the bar. A sudden silence descended and Catrin glanced up to find herself looking into a pair of inky eyes. He was staring very hard and it took a moment or two for her to realise that his narrowed gaze was directed at her. If she hadn't been standing with her back against a wall, she might have thought he was looking at someone else. But he wasn't.

He was looking at her.

His eyes were travelling over her in a way which if it had been anyone else, Catrin might have found offensive. But with him it didn't feel a bit offensive. With him, it felt…natural. As if she had been waiting all her life for him to look at her that way. Every vein in her body seemed to open wider to let the ever-quickening pulse of blood through. She could feel her breasts growing heavy and the palms of her hands getting clammy. Her reaction confused her. It scared her and excited her. It made her words come out sounding more clipped than usual, although nothing could disguise the soft lilt of her Welsh accent.

'Can I help you, sir?'

There was a pause. His eyes were still narrowed. His voice was low and caressing. 'I suspect you can help me in ways you haven't even begun to dream of,' he said, in an accent she'd never heard before.

'I'm sorry?'

He shook his head, the way people did when they were trying to clear their ears after they'd been swimming. As if he'd just found himself in a place he hadn't expected to be. 'Some coffee, I think.'

Catrin raised her eyebrows and spoke to him in exactly the same way as she might speak to any young farmer who had taken temporary leave of their manners. 'I usually respond better to the word "please".'

He smiled then, before looking at her with a hard and playful gleam in his eyes. The way a cat looked at a bird which was high up in a tree. 'Please.'

Afterwards she would discover that it had been impulse which had brought him into the old-fashioned hotel, leaving a whole fleet of accompanying bodyguards kicking their heels outside. He told her later that fate must have lured him there, because he had been meant to meet her. And that she was the most beautiful woman he had ever seen.

Of course, she hadn't known any of this as he sat down and began to sip his coffee and asked what her name was. And although she rarely socialised with customers, she found herself standing on the other side of the bar talking to him—or, rather, listening to what he was saying about wind farms, which was the reason for his visit to the area. At that point she still hadn't discovered that he was a sultan who ruled a vast area of oil-rich land and was wealthy in a way which was outside her understanding.

All she knew was that he spoke like no one else she'd ever heard. His accented voice made her think of velvet and stone. He exuded an air of self-possession she found irresistible. And he flirted in a way she knew was dangerous, but which didn't stop her from responding. She would have defied any woman on the planet not to have responded.

'I suppose people must tell you all the time that your eyes are very beautiful,' he said, making her stomach flip as he sucked on a coffee-dunked lump of sugar. 'They are the colour of a cactus.'

'A cactus!' She looked at him perplexed, and pursed her lips together. 'A horrible prickly cactus?'

'That is the general perception of the plant, yes,' he agreed, his voice dipping into a silken caress. 'But it happens to be one of the world's most underrated examples of vegetation. Not only can they can store water and survive in the most arduous of conditions, but they provide nourishment and have many medicinal properties.' He smiled again. 'As well as producing flowers of quite breathtaking beauty.'

Rapt now, Catrin nodded. His words sounded… incredible. Like poetry. She wanted to hear more of them. They made her want him to whisper things. Things which weren't about plants. Things about her. Things about…

Her cheeks were burning as she walked to the other end of the bar and took ages pulling a pint of beer for another customer, because it was wrong to think that way. She knew that there were two types of men and this one was the wrong type. Hadn't her mother always told her to look in the mirror if she needed any proof about the wrong type?

'Why are you blushing?' he asked softly.

She looked up and suddenly she could think of nothing but him. Common sense and playing safe seemed like quite reasonable endeavours for other people, but not for her. Everything she'd ever been told about handsome, dangerous men began to trickle away, like the froth on top of the pint she was pulling. She looked deep into his eyes and wondered what it would be like to kiss him.

'I've never actually seen a flowering cactus,' she said.

He smiled, and there was the heartbeat of a pause. 'Haven't you?'

The next day, a delivery was made. At first it looked like a regular florist's delivery—with its shiny cellophane and fancy ribbon. It was only when she opened it that Catrin discovered the succulent green leaves of a cactus on which bloomed miniature petalled suns, in shades of cerise and rose. She'd never been sent flowers before and she'd certainly never been given anything like this. The originality and unexpectedness of the gesture stabbed at her heart with a fierce kind of joy.

She guessed it was inevitable that she should agree to have dinner with him. What she didn't anticipate—and which afterwards surprised her as much as him—was ending up in Murat's four-poster bed overlooking Bala Lake that very same night.

It was wild. Or rather, *she* was wild. She had never known something could feel so good. Her hands splayed eagerly over his naked body as he kissed her and she clung to him as greedily as a barnacle to a rock. At first, he seemed a little taken aback by her passion, but the moan he gave as he thrust deep inside her made her feel almost powerful.

The next bit wasn't great because it hurt and because he was furious that she'd omitted to mention the small matter of her virginity.

'Why me?' he demanded afterwards, as if giving someone your innocence were a burden rather than a gift.

'Because...because I'd waited for someone who knew what they were doing and you fitted the bill. I wanted it be fantastic. And it was. Why?' She rolled over, resting her elbows on his chest and looking straight into his eyes. 'Is it important?'

'Of course it is,' he said. 'I'm not in the habit of seducing virgins. Their dreams are still intact.'

'Too late,' she teased, her mouth trailing over his hair-roughened chest.

He did it to her again. And again. And the third time she lay trembling in his arms, kissing the same spot on his shoulder, over and over again. He was stroking her hair and when she spoke, her voice was dazed.

'That was...amazing.'

'I know,' he said, running the tip of his tongue over her ear. 'They say it takes a little practice for a woman to orgasm.'

'Then I think it's very important I keep practising,' she said solemnly and he laughed.

'You are a curious mixture,' he observed slowly, 'of the unworldly and the seasoned.'

'And is that a good thing or a bad thing?'

'I can't quite decide,' came his answer. 'All I know is that I find you quite enchanting and I'm not sure that I'm prepared to let you go.'

She snuggled up to him. 'Then don't,' she whispered. 'Keep on holding me, just like that.'

They were both talking about different things,

of course. As someone who had learnt never to pro-
ject, Catrin was thinking about the glorious present,
while—unusually for him—Murat was speculating
about the future. She said goodbye, telling herself
that she would probably never see him again—but
to her astonishment he returned the following week,
when she had two whole days off.

'You see,' he said lightly. 'I just can't keep away
from you.'

She made no attempt to hide her delight as he
pulled her into his arms. For the first time in her
life she understood the meaning of the expression
*walking on air*. She found herself thanking some
unknown fate, which had brought her to the other
side of Wales, leaving her to conduct her love affair
without fear of her mother turning up and creating
a scene.

But that was something else she liked about
Murat. He wasn't interested in her family, or her
background. Why would he be, when this was never
meant to be anything but temporary? It meant that
she didn't have to go through the agonising torture
of explaining what her home life had been like.

They booked into the same hotel overlooking Bala
Lake and for two whole days they scarcely left the
bedroom. She wondered how she was going to cope
when he went back to his other life. His real life. His
desert life, which he'd told her about and which had
no room for someone like her.

She tried not to think about it, but it was impossible not to. It was hard to equate her fierce lover with

a man who ruled a vast kingdom and rode a black
stallion over hot and arid sands. She ran her fingertips through the rich silk of his ebony hair and tried
not to think about losing him.

Did he guess at her thoughts, or did he read it in
her eyes? Was that why he came out with his extraordinary proposition on that last afternoon, before
he was due to drive back to London for a business
dinner?

'Come away with me,' he said, pulling on the
jacket of his elegant Italian suit.

She blinked. 'Where?'

'To London. I have an apartment there. You could
live there.'

'With you?'

He gave a funny kind of smile. 'Well, sometimes.'

If only she hadn't been so naïve. If only she'd
realised what she was getting herself into, and that
women like her were never offered *permanence*. The
only permanence in Murat's life was his palace and
his busy schedule in Qurhah. The trips he made to
England were fleeting and irregular and he certainly
wasn't offering her a conventional relationship.

But she wasn't used to convention—or relationships. She was a stranger to commitment and she
told herself she didn't do emotion. Emotion brought
chaos—and she'd had enough chaos to last a lifetime.

She thought of turning him down and then asked
herself why she would do something that insane.
And really, what alternative did she have, when the
thought of him walking out of her life made her feel

as if someone were trying to hack open her heart with a blunt chisel?

That was when and how she had become a rich man's mistress. She had gone to London to be with Murat and slowly but surely her independence had begun to ebb away. The job she'd found at a big hotel soon proved incompatible with her new life, because quickly she learned that was the first rule of being a mistress.

You always needed to be available.

Murat told her that his world was full of pressure and that she—uniquely—soothed his frazzled nerves. He liked her being there when he arrived in England and didn't want her working shifts and wasting precious time when she could be with *him*. He waved aside her initial protests that she couldn't possibly use his charge card. He told her that he had more than enough money for both of them. That she was, in effect, acting as his housekeeper since she made his apartment feel like a home.

So she had let him slide that plastic card into her brand-new designer wallet. Just as she'd let him kit her out in silks and satins and started having her hair done regularly at one of London's most exclusive hair salons.

She hadn't thought about how long it would last. She hadn't thought beyond each glorious day. But she had started to like him more and more. And that was when she had started trying to make it perfect. The perfect relationship to make up for her very imperfect childhood.

She learned that expensive fabrics felt better against the skin than cheap ones. She learned to enjoy visiting the spa in preparation for his visits, and having her body pummelled and anointed with buttery creams. She learned to fill his many absences with the short courses available to rich women with plenty of time on their hands. She did musical appreciation and flower arrangement. She got herself a *cordon bleu* certificate and learned about different wines. She found that she had a real passion for the history of art. Suddenly, she was getting herself an education.

He introduced her to first one colleague, and then another. Sometimes they brought their wives, sometimes their mistresses. She discovered that her time at the Hindmarsh Hotel had proved very useful, because she could talk to almost anyone with an easy charm. She learnt to read up about people before meeting them and to impress them with her knowledge of wind farms, or fracking—or whatever was currently occupying the business life of her royal lover.

In a way, she was teaching herself to become the perfect consort of a powerful man, but there was no prospect of such a permanent role. Not for her. He needed to marry a pure-blooded royal; a bona fide desert princess. He had been very honest about that, right from the start.

They had understood each other, or so she'd thought. And because there had been no lies or pretence, she'd thought it would be easy to accept the rigid terms of their relationship.

And it was. At least, at the beginning it was. It was love which was the killer. Love which made her want more than she was ever going to get...

'Cat?'

Murat's shuddered use of her name brought her thoughts crashing back to the present and Catrin opened her eyes to find his face inches away from hers. She could see the gleam of his black eyes and feel the warmth of his breath as his naked body melded close to hers, her breasts flattened against his hair-roughened chest.

'What is it, my beauty?' he questioned, his breathing unsteady as he ran his hand possessively down over the curve of her hip. 'You were miles away.'

No way was she going to admit to inhabiting the dangerous landscape of the past—or tell him about all the stupid doubts which had been crowding her mind. She shook her head and pressed her body closer, feeling his hardness pushing insistently against her wet heat.

'I'm here now,' she whispered. 'And I'm all yours.'

But for how long? she wondered.

Parting her thighs, he thrust deep inside her—but even as her body opened up to welcome him, she could feel another hint of darkness closing around her heart.

# CHAPTER THREE

'OKAY. SO HOW about this? Does it work for you?' Walking across the room on sky-high heels, Catrin stopped in front of the TV soccer game which was currently engrossing the Sultan. 'Am I suitably dressed for this dinner with Niccolo Da Conti?'

Either it had been a boring game or she must have put on exactly the right dress, because Murat took his eye off the ball and focused on her instead, a slow smile of appreciation curving his lips.

He was wearing nothing but a small towel wrapped around his hips and his hair was still damp from the shower he'd taken directly after making love to her. Catrin could still feel the faint flush to her skin, together with the still galloping race of her heart. She swallowed. It had been some homecoming.

'Turn around,' he said softly.

She obeyed his command, aware of the wash of air over her bare thighs as she turned, because beneath her delicate lilac dress she was wearing the stockings he always insisted on.

Usually she enjoyed this deliberate little show, which was staged to allow Murat to be openly voyeuristic. Sometimes he might ask to see the tops of her stockings and she would tease him with a provocative flash, like an old-fashioned cancan dancer. Whatever it was he wanted, she did her best to oblige. It was another of the lessons Murat had taught her: that a man need never stray if he had a generous lover at home.

But she still couldn't seem to shake off those doubts which had been bugging her all day. They were sliding over her skin like snails and leaving a trail of something cold behind. She could sense that something in her life was changing and she wasn't sure what it was. She remembered that odd look on his face when he'd been making love to her earlier.

Was he growing tired of her?

Her pulse picked up an unsteady beat, because she didn't *want* anything to change. This situation wasn't perfect—she knew that. These snatched moments with Murat were never enough—but she liked her life as it was. There were definite advantages to being with a man who was emotionally off-limits. At least they didn't waste time with rows or unreasonable demands. And if she disregarded this stupid *love* idea, then hadn't she landed herself a pretty good deal, on balance?

But if Murat was tiring of her…

Catrin thought of the alternatives which lay open to her, trying to imagine where she would go from here. Because hadn't she allowed her modest ambitions to fall by the wayside since moving in with Murat? What about that little tea room in the Welsh mountains which had once been her dream? The great idea that she would bake home-made cakes and sell them to hungry mountaineers, but which now didn't seem quite so appealing.

Wasn't the truth of it that living with Murat had subtly helped change her dreams, and now the thought of any kind of life without him was simply... unimaginable? Their lives had become interwoven, but the Sultan definitely called the shots. Sometimes she felt like a young sapling which was being bent by a warm and powerful wind. Like now.

So when he told her to turn around, she did—with a graceful twirl which made the silk chiffon of her dress swirl round her like a ballet dancer.

'You mean, like that?' she said lightly.

'I mean, just like that.'

He was looking at her as she imagined a leopard might look at a passing antelope before clamping its jaws around it. 'Not too long?' she probed. 'Or too short?'

'I could think of many ways to describe what you're wearing, though some of them might shock your tender Welsh ears.' His soccer game forgotten, Murat lolled back against the cushions littering the sofa. 'It's perfect. As are you. And I only have to look at you to want you.'

'Again?'

'Always.' His black eyes grew smoky and she saw his thumb slide down over the white towel to halt at the rapidly hardening ridge at his groin. 'Do you want to come over here and suck me?'

Catrin could do nothing to prevent the desire which shivered down her spine, but in that instant she recognised that something really *had* changed. She was appalled to realise that usually she would have said yes, like some obedient woman from the harem. She would have gone over there and plea-sured him and then probably had to go and change her dress and reapply her make-up.

But the thought of doing that suddenly left her cold. Maybe her mother's words had affected her more than she'd thought. Maybe her own troubled thoughts were more potent than she had imagined.

Shaking her head, she walked over to the win-dow seat and sat down on it, pushing her knees close together because she didn't want him to see that they were trembling. 'Not now, Murat—if you don't mind.'

'And if I do?' he drawled lazily.

She didn't rise to it; just kept that same rather se-rene smile on her lips. 'I'd rather hear a little more about Niccolo. Tell me again how you met.'

He eyed her speculatively, as if deciding how much to tell her.

'Da Conti is what is known as an *international playboy*,' he said. 'We met on the ski slopes some years ago and our interests have merged from time to time. There were a group of us who used to race together, which included the Formula One champion,

Luis Martinez.' He gave a dry laugh. 'We were all very young and a little…wild.'

She tried not to react, because sometimes Murat had told her things about his past which she wished he'd kept quiet. But sometimes you found yourself blurting out a question, even if you had no desire to hear the answer. 'Does that mean you've shared women?'

'Never intentionally and never at the same time.' He shrugged his broad shoulders in a gesture which Catrin supposed was intended to be apologetic—though at that moment it seemed more like a boast. She wondered if it was intended to remind her that women regularly flung themselves at him and were always trying to lure him into their beds. Maybe he wanted to emphasise that there were plenty of candidates all too eager to take her place…

'How very commendable of you,' she said.

'Not really. You know me, Cat—I don't like sharing anything, but sharing a woman with your friends is a recipe for disaster.' He smiled. 'Niccolo has been threatening to go into the oil business for as long as I can remember and he has finally bought himself an oil well in Zaminzar—'

'That's the country which borders the eastern side of your own, isn't it?'

His eyes narrowed. 'How do you know that?'

She found his sudden change of tone vaguely unsettling and suddenly Catrin forgot all the 'rules' she usually applied when she was spending precious time with Murat. She forgot that she always tried to be like a soothing balm and never to stress him. All her good intentions flew straight out of the window as an unfamiliar feeling of belligerence began to bubble up inside her.

'You mentioned it to me yourself,' she said. 'Sometimes you actually let your two worlds collide and sometimes you actually talk to me about your other life. Your desert life,' she added, more tightly than she had intended.

He studied her thoughtfully. 'That sounds like a complaint.'

'Not really. It's the way it is and I accept that. I'm just stating a fact, Murat—which is a bright thing to do. You're the one who told me a person should always face facts.'

'Did I say that?' He stood up, but the sudden hardening of his mouth showed his displeasure. As if the evening wasn't panning out the way he wanted it to.

And suddenly Catrin felt exactly the same way. This wasn't panning out the way *she* had planned it either. She had wanted the atmosphere to be warm and giving—not filled with the spiky little barbs which they seemed to be at hurling at one another.

*You're ruining what little time you have with him. So stop it.*

Swallowing down her anxiety, she forced a friendly smile onto her lips. 'Where…where are we eating tonight?'

Murat looked at her and an unfamiliar sense of remorse washed over him as he saw the sudden fear in her eyes. He had often been accused of cruelty by

lovers in the past, but he didn't set out to be cruel—
and certainly not to Catrin, who was the longest last-
ing of all his lovers. He just knew his limitations; it
was as simple as that.

Emotion left him cold and duty was his lifeblood.
He had no desire to indulge in something as dull as
analysing his feelings, for his demanding position as
Sultan left him no time for such self-serving pursuits.
His father had drummed into him what was expected
of a desert king. He knew the future which had been
mapped out for him and he accepted the strictures
it placed on him. He thought Cat had accepted them
too—for he had laid down his terms for the relationship from the very beginning. Yet hadn't it already
lasted longer than anticipated—and weren't questions now being asked in Qurhah about the Sultan's
English lover and her significance in his life?

He had told his advisors that his private life was
exactly that and he did not intend discussing it. And
fortunately, his exalted position and power and the
sheer force of his personality had guaranteed their
immediate silence. But deep down he had known that
he could not continue with this double life much longer—especially now that his sister was married and
heavy with child. His filial responsibilities had been
discharged and now it was his own marital future
which was giving his country cause for concern. His
people wanted their sultan to marry and they were
eager for him to produce an heir. Hadn't that been
why he had agreed to the latest attempt at matchmak-

ing, even though something inside him had told him
from the start that it was destined to fail?

His mouth tightened as he looked at her trembling
lips and knew he should tell her.

But when?

He remembered the old saying which his palace
tutor had taught him. This year? Next year? Some
time? Never?

He certainly didn't want his sweet Welsh lover to
wear that look of hurt which her smile couldn't quite
disguise, or for her beautiful green eyes to darken
when she looked at him like that.

He walked over to where she sat on the window
seat, before bending down to brush his lips over hers.
'You know that I would prefer to spend the evening
here with you and only you—but this meeting is important. And it gives me an invaluable opportunity
to talk football—since nobody appreciates the sport
as much as an Italian.'

'Which I agree is much too good an opportunity
to pass up,' she said. 'If only I could remember the
offside rule, then maybe I could talk football, too.'

He relaxed a little as he saw that her uncharacter-
istic sulk was already subsiding, and he tangled his
fingers in the silky fall of her hair. 'I'd love to see Da
Conti's face if you started talking about the offside
rule! And if I can't persuade you to rub me dry, then
I guess I'd better go and get dressed. I won't be long.'

Catrin sat staring into space while Murat changed
and he reappeared just as the peal of the doorbell
echoed through the apartment. Outside the heavily

fortified door stood two bodyguards, who accompanied them down in the elevator. Murat's bullet-proof car was waiting in the street, with a second vehicle ready to follow close behind. The whole operation happened with a swift smoothness which Catrin now took for granted.

Her lover had riches beyond the dreams of most men, but it was difficult to get to do anything 'normal' with him. Going anywhere meant having a whole team of accompanying guards, which always made people stare. The only place where they could be really private was tucked away inside his apartment. He told her that he'd eaten in fancy restaurants all his life and they bored him. That he'd rather spend time alone with her. At the time his declaration had flattered her, but now she was beginning to wonder whether she should have asked for more.

Catrin frowned. Had she been crazy to settle for what he had offered her—or rather, for what he *hadn't* offered her? Had she secretly been thinking that one day he might change his mind about love and marriage?

'We're here,' said Murat, his voice breaking her racing thoughts as the car drew up outside a discreet restaurant.

It was one of those places so full of important people that few arrivals warranted a second glance. Murat did, of course—but Catrin was used to him drawing the eye wherever they went. She guessed his raw sex appeal, coupled with the unconscious arrogance which accompanied royal power, made for a pretty irresistible combination.

She felt increasingly edgy as they began to walk through the restaurant, where Niccolo Da Conti was already seated at a table towards the back of the room. Catrin could see a man with ruffled dark hair and a lazy smile, leaning back while a waiter poured him a glass of champagne. Close beside him was a long-legged blonde, wearing a tiny dress of silver mesh, which gleamed against the caramel glow of her skin. Her glossy silver fingernails were splayed possessively over one of Niccolo's thighs, as if they were glued to that hard and muscular surface.

Catrin was smiling as they approached the table, but her lingering disquiet was making her palms grow clammy. Calm down, she told herself fiercely. Nothing has changed. Everything is just the way it has always been.

'Murat,' said Niccolo Da Conti, shaking off the blonde as he rose to his feet, his two hands out-stretched in greeting. 'How is my favourite Middle-Eastern potentate? Would you like me to bow?'

'I would much rather you didn't.' Murat laughed. 'Two of my bodyguards are seated discreetly a few tables away and they like me to remain as incognito as possible.'

'*You*, incognito? I don't think so. Every eye in the place was on you from the moment you walked in. I've never known it to be any different.' Niccolo turned and smiled. 'And you must be Catrin. I can't believe we haven't met before—but I believe Murat keeps you tucked away so that nobody else can get close. Looking at you now, I can see exactly why. It's good to meet you.'

'Stop flirting, Nic,' said Murat, 'and introduce us to the lady.'

The lady was Niccolo's Norwegian girlfriend, Lise, who, while looking exactly like a supermodel, turned out to be a financial wizard working in mergers and acquisitions. It was difficult not to be impressed by a woman who had made her first million by the age of twenty-five. And even harder not to feel a little second rate in the shining light of all that bright, blonde beauty. Catrin gave a slightly nervous smile as she sat down.

'So what do you do, Catrin?' Lise questioned, once drinks had been poured and the two men were engaged in a complicated conversation about wind farms.

Beneath the steady gaze of the other woman's eyes, Catrin tried not to feel awkward. She always hated this bit. What could she possibly say in response to a question which everyone asked, wherever they went? That she used to work in the hotel industry until Murat had put his foot down and told her that her unsociable hours were keeping them apart and he wasn't prepared to tolerate it?

And she had agreed. She had given up work because it had seemed crazy not to. Why would you waste your time working for peanuts, when your wealthy sultan was at home, drumming his fingers impatiently as he waited for you to finish your shift?

'I used to work in the hospitality industry,' she said. 'But not at the moment.'

'Gosh. Lucky you,' said Lise lightly. 'I'd give anything not to be ruled by the demands of the early-morning wake-up call.'

They ordered food and wine though Catrin stuck to water, just as she always did. They talked politics and about America's enduring love affair with the British royal family, before the two men started discussing oil prices.

Lise turned to Catrin, elevating her brows in a comical expression.

'Isn't this where we zone out?' she questioned. 'And talk about the stuff women like to talk about?'

'I guess so,' said Catrin, though another faint flicker of disquiet fluttered down her spine.

At first they kept the conversation strictly neutral. Lise wanted to know the name of Catrin's hairdresser and that bit was easy. Then she admired her lapis lazuli locket and asked where she'd got it from. Catrin ran her fingertips over the deep blue stone.

'Murat bought it for my birthday.'

'Did he? He has very good taste.'

'Yes.' Catrin felt the cool brush of the stone as it dangled between her breasts. She remembered the touch of Murat's fingers the first time he had clipped it around her neck. She swallowed. 'He has excellent taste.'

'So I understand. Have you two been together a long time?'

'Just over...' Her fingers falling away from the

necklace, Catrin picked up her glass and wished—as sometimes she did—that she possessed enough courage to drink a glass of wine. Because wouldn't a drink take the edge off these gnawing feelings of unease? Wasn't that why most people drank? *Most* people, she reminded herself as a shudder of memory whispered over her skin. 'Just over a year,' she said.

'Mmm. Longer than I thought.' There was a moment of silence before Lise slanted her a speculative look. 'You are a very pragmatic woman, I think.'

Catrin felt a little taken aback at such an unexpected character assessment. It seemed a strange thing to be told by somebody she'd only just met. She glanced across the table towards Murat, but by now he was busy talking soccer with Niccolo and completely engrossed by the subject.

'What makes you say that?' she questioned.

'Oh, you know.' Lise shrugged. 'It can't be easy for you.'

'I'm sorry?'

'All the interminable pressure on Murat to find a suitable bride.'

Catrin's smile didn't slip, even though the word *suitable* reminded her of all the things she wasn't. All the things she could never be. 'If you're talking about Princess Sara—I know all about her,' she said, wondering if she sounded as defensive as she felt. 'I know she was promised to the Sultan, but the wedding was called off. And Murat was fine with it. In fact, he was more than fine.'

'But I thought…'

Lise's voice tailed off and she applied her attention to her starter, suddenly stabbing at the slice of smoked salmon as if it were alive on the plate.

During the pause which followed, Catrin felt the frightened leap of her heart. She felt as Eve must have done as she looked at the forbidden apple, unable to resist the temptation of something which was guaranteed to bring nothing but trouble. 'What did you think?' she asked quietly.

Lise managed to shake her head without a single strand of her blonde hair moving. 'Honestly, it's nothing.'

'Please,' said Catrin. She gave another of those convincing little smiles she seemed to have become so good at lately. 'I'd really like to know.'

Her gaze darting over towards the two men, as if checking they weren't listening, Lise shrugged. 'It's just that I've learned quite a bit about the desert regions since Niccolo acquired his new toy.'

'New toy?' repeated Catrin blankly.

'His oil well. Which makes a change from an airline or a football team, but which means he spends more time in Zaminzar than I'd like. ' Lise pulled a face. 'It's much too hot there, and people seem to object if you show off even the tiniest bit of your body.'

Catrin thought this was a bit like complaining that anyone travelling to Alaska was advised to wear warm clothes, but she didn't say anything. She wanted to know why Lise had called her 'pragmatic' and managed to make it sound like an insult in the process.

'So what exactly have you heard?' she questioned. 'About Murat?'

Lise put her fork down; her smoked salmon untouched. 'That his people are eager for him to produce an heir. That they consider the dynasty to be unstable as long as there is no direct bloodline.'

'I think that's always been the case.'

'And that's why he's been in Zaminzar these past few weeks,' continued Lise. 'He has been meeting with the king's daughter there, with the question of marriage very much in mind. You knew about that, of course? Apparently, she's quite a beauty.'

Catrin felt faint. Yellow-white spots danced before her eyes. She became aware of the sudden rush of blood to her head and the sound of roaring in her ears, but somehow she kept her smile in place. That stupid smile, which meant nothing.

'Yes, I'd heard something along those lines,' she said carelessly.

'You had?' Lise's mouth opened wide, like a camera lens. 'And you're okay with it?'

For a moment Catrin was tempted to tell the truth. To say: *Of course I didn't know that! And even if I did, do you really think I'd be okay with it?* Knowing that the man she loved was actively courting another woman *without even bothering to tell her*?

What would Lise say if she bellowed out her pain and distress in the middle of the crowded restaurant and admitted that she felt a fool? Worse than a fool. She felt like the kind of woman who would accept whatever scraps a man was prepared to fling her way. Who would take whatever was on offer and that would be good enough—because hadn't it been that way all her life? Had she become so used to accepting second best that she had carried it on into her adult life, and then thought it would make her *happy*?

Knowing she had no right to take out her distress on Lise—for that would simply be shooting the messenger—she drank some water, and shrugged.

'Of course I'm okay with that,' she said. 'It's no great secret. I've known right from the start that there was never going to be any future for me and Murat.'

Lise wore the same kind of expression as somebody who had slowed down on a motorway to survey the wreckage of a recent accident. *'Really?'*

'Really.' Where *had* she learned this smile? Catrin wondered. Had she been a magician's assistant in a former life? 'I've always known that the Sultan would have to marry a woman of pure, royal blood and that woman was never going to be me. That's why neither Murat nor I have ever tied each other down with any kind of commitment.'

The words sounded so convincing that she very nearly convinced herself. She managed to get them out as smoothly as if she had been commenting on the quality of the scallops, which now lay cold and congealing on her plate. And wasn't it good to say them, rather than letting them build up inside her like a slow poison?

'I'm with you there, and I'll drink to that,' said Lise, raising her glass in mocking salute. 'Because getting Niccolo to commit is like getting blood from a stone.'

But the false camaraderie between her and Lise made Catrin suddenly feel *pathetic*. As if they were a band of desperate women dating these two very eligible bachelors and waiting for them to commit.

Was that what she had become?

For a moment she experienced the strange, telescoping sensation of looking at herself from the outside. Of seeing herself as others saw her. A woman in an expensive dress without a job. A woman whose life was spent waiting for a man she increasingly saw less of. It was not a pretty picture and she felt the sour taste of self-disgust. She found herself asking just how long she was prepared to continue with a situation like this? Until Murat *did* find himself a wife?

Pushing her food around the plate, she somehow managed to get through the rest of the meal. In fact, she did more than get through it. For a woman who had just found out that her lover had been actively seeking another bride, she thought her behaviour was exemplary. If medals were being awarded for indifference in the face of emotional turmoil, she would have come out with a shiny gold one. Nobody would have guessed from her attitude that she and Lise hadn't spent the time discussing manicures, or recent films they had seen.

At one point she laughed so loudly at a joke Niccolo made that Murat sent a frowning look of disapproval icing across the table towards her. Which only made her want to laugh harder and louder.

He didn't say a word until they were in the car on the way home, but when he turned to her it was with an unmistakable look of disapproval on his face.

'So what got into you over dinner?' he said, his forefinger tapping against his lips, like a teacher awaiting the answer to a question. 'What merited the rather hysterical outbursts?'

For a moment Catrin didn't reply, because she hadn't got as far as working out what she was going to say to him. She thought of a million responses she could make to his cutting remark and—God help her—wasn't there still a part of her which wanted to smooth it all over and make as if nothing had happened? To pretend that Lise had revealed nothing at all and therefore nothing had changed.

But it *had* changed. She knew that. The rot had set in and it had started before Lise had spilled the beans. It had started the moment she had acknowledged that she was in love with him, because love changed everything. It made your heart hurt. It made you long for more—for things you knew you could never have. She couldn't put her arms around him and ignore the faceless princess who might soon become his bride. She had to face facts, just as she'd boasted to him about doing earlier that evening.

It occurred to her that she hadn't even questioned the truth of Lise's statement, because she knew it *was* true. It explained so much about Murat's behaviour which she hadn't dared examine before. The longer gaps between his visits. The way he often seemed *preoccupied* when he was with her.

She knew she should wait until they got back to the apartment to confront him. She knew it wasn't appropriate to raise her voice in anger, when the Qurhahian driver might conceivably overhear. But Catrin couldn't stop the feelings which were washing over her, no matter how much she tried to tell herself that she was being unreasonable. All her suppressed emotions came bubbling out and there didn't seem a thing she could do to stop them.

'What got into me?' she questioned and her voice was shaking with rage. 'I'll tell you exactly! Lise says you've been actively seeking a bride. In fact, that you've been interviewing one over this past month. In Zaminzar. Meeting with some beautiful princess.'

'Cat,' he said warningly. 'Not here.'

'Yes! Right here. Right now. No wonder you got so defensive when I started talking about Zaminzar earlier.' She could feel the bile rising in her throat and suddenly there was no holding it back. 'I'm curious to know what form of interviewing technique you were using with this beautiful princess. Were you having sex with your bride-to-be, Murat, just before coming to London to have hot sex with *me*?'

# CHAPTER FOUR

MURAT FELT HIS hackles rising as he stared into Cat's angry face because he wasn't used to being challenged—not by her. Not by anyone. And especially not in full earshot of his driver.

Yet he wondered realistically how much longer he could have kept this a secret. The entire desert community had been buzzing with the latest attempt to marry off one of its most eligible bachelors and there were plans for yet more meetings in the pipeline. It felt like a heavy burden of guilt he'd been carrying around for too long and, in some perverse way, didn't he almost *welcome* its arrival?

'Did you?' she was saying, in a reckless tone he'd never heard her use before. 'Have sex with her before you came to me?'

In the shadowed light of the car, he could see her lips trembling and he felt a brief, sharp pang of guilt. But behind the screen sat his driver and next to him a bodyguard and, although they'd all been trained to turn a blind eye to the Sultan's private life, he had no intention of discussing his sex life in front of any of them.

'Let's talk about it when we get back.'

'I want to talk about it *now*.'

'I said, *no*, Cat,' he snapped. 'How dare you berate me with all the finesse of a common fishwife? I am not having this conversation with you in public and providing some kind of sideshow for the benefit of my staff. So you'd better hold back your questions until we get home—because I don't intend to answer any of them.'

Deliberately, he turned his head away, the imperious wave of his hand reinforcing his intention not to respond. He told himself that she had overstepped the mark, but his determination to turn away from her stemmed from more than anger at her insubordination.

The truth was that he didn't want to have to look at her reproachful expression, nor to anticipate where this conversation was heading—because he suspected he wouldn't like the answer. He told himself that he was doing the only thing a man in his position *could* do. He was thinking of his country. Of his bloodline—one of the longest and most noble of all the desert states. He thought of his people—of the deprivations they had known. He thought of his land's chequered and bloody history, and his mouth hardened.

He knew what he had to do because duty had been drummed into him from the moment he had been old enough to understand the meaning of the word.

He knew that he needed to take a royal bride and to produce a male child, as his father had done—and his father before him. He needed to pave the way for the Al Maisan dynasty to continue into time immemorial.

In theory, such a task should have been easy. He was now thirty-six and ready for the responsibilities of fatherhood, in a way he had never been ready before. The princess of Zaminzar—Aleya was her name—was beautiful and cultured. She could speak four languages and her comely hips looked as if they could bear him many sons. She ticked many of the right boxes, as they often said in the west. Some, but not all.

Yet even though this latest attempt had failed, there would be others—and he would not feel guilty about something which Cat had always known would happen. *He* was the Sultan, carrying out the role expected of him, and he would not be reprimanded by his mistress!

They sat in simmering silence until the car reached his apartment and the atmosphere during the elevator ride to the penthouse was similarly tense. As soon as he'd shut the apartment door, he saw Cat kicking off her high heels and hurling them across the room before turning on him, her face contorted with anger.

'The truth, Murat,' she said, her voice shaking. 'I want the truth.'

For the first time Murat felt an unfamiliar wave of uncertainty about how to handle her, because Cat didn't do angry. Cat did sweet and willing and compliant, and if she had been her usual sweet and accommodating self he might have…

Might have, what?

Was he really fooling himself that he could have talked or kissed his way out of *this*?

Angry himself now, he walked into the sitting room and stared out of the window at the faint sprinkle of stars which glittered above the treetops.

'Murat?' she said, from behind him. 'Are you going to answer my question?'

He turned before she had a chance to compose herself and he saw on her face something which speared at his conscience like a rusty blade. Because despite everything—the unmistakable flare of hope was alive in her beautiful eyes. And didn't they say that hope was the one thing which every human being clung to, no matter what the circumstances?

She wanted him to tell her that the interfering girlfriend of Niccolo Da Conti had been wrong. She wanted him to tell her that it had all been a mistake. That he was not seeking any woman other than her.

Except that he couldn't.

He couldn't lie to her.

He had always told her the truth.

He looked her squarely in the eye. 'What exactly do you want to know?'

He could see her momentary hesitation—as if she recognised that there could be no going back from this. *So don't ask me,* he prayed silently. *Let me take you to bed and kiss away the questions. Let's forget tonight ever happened and just enjoy what is within our grasp.*

'Have you been seeing someone you're intending to marry?'

He made an impatient movement with his hands. 'My whole adult life has been spent meeting prospective wives,' he said. 'You know that. I've explained it to you. I told you about Princess Sara. I told you all about the others—the ones I deemed unsuitable.'

'That's just a clever way of avoiding my question. A simple yes or no will suffice.' She licked her lips, as if playing for time. 'Have you been courting another woman?'

There was a pause.

'I've been in discussion with the King of Zaminzar's daughter, yes,' he said eventually. 'With a view to marriage, yes again.'

'And did you…did you sleep with her?'

Her question was so quiet that he had to strain his ears to hear it and Murat glowered in response. He wondered if she was aware that she was severely testing his patience, and that he would not be interrogated like a common thief. Yet once again something in her green eyes smote at his conscience and he found himself shaking his head.

'No, I did not. And I am shocked that you should ask me such a question when I've told you that I never sleep with more than one woman at the same time.'

'*You're* shocked?' she echoed and then shook her head. 'You are unbelievable, Murat. *Unbelievable.*'

Murat could feel the slow smoulder of rage building up inside him and he let it come. He let it heat up his blood and his skin, the way it did just before he rode into battle. Because rage obliterated pretty much everything else, and it was much easier to live with than regret.

'You do not own me,' he said. 'And you do not have exclusive rights to me. Even if I had wanted to have sex with her, I couldn't have done so—because the kind of woman I will eventually marry is not the kind of woman who will give her body freely to a man.'

There was a long and disbelieving silence as she stared at him.

'Unlike me, you mean?' she questioned.

He shrugged. 'Maybe I shouldn't have said that.'

'Or maybe you should. Maybe it's good for me to hear you admit that there are two types of women. The type who become wives and the type who become mistresses.'

'But I never promised you marriage, Cat,' he said. 'I made that clear from the start. I told you that our relationship could never be anything other than temporary. Didn't I? Or did you think that my words were empty?'

Cat stared at him, feeling some of her anger evaporate as she forced herself to take stock of what he was saying. Yes, he had told her all those things; right from the start he'd been honest with her. He'd told her that she could be his lover, but never his bride. And what had she done? She'd reassured him that she was perfectly okay with that. She'd even managed to convince herself that theirs was the kind of relationship she wanted. That she was modern enough not to care about convention. That she was so messed up from her past that she didn't want a relationship with all the normal rules.

But somewhere along the way something unexpected had happened. She had started to care for him, and that had never been part of the plan. She'd been so eager to hold onto him that she had moulded herself into the sort of woman she thought he wanted her to be. Like some kind of sexy geisha, she had put his needs before her own every time. Always smiling; never complaining; she had accepted whatever came her way.

So how could she now object to his behaviour, when all he had been doing was what he had warned her about all along?

*He had been looking for a wife.*

Of course he had.

How stupid she must seem for trying to rail against the inevitable—she was like the foolish king who had tried to turn back the tide. What did she think was going to happen—that Murat would defy his proud destiny and hitch his star to a working-class girl from the Welsh valleys? An illegitimate girl with a hopeless drunk for a mother?

She realised that he was still looking at her and she drew in a deep breath, trying to claw back some of the dignity which she had let slip away. 'Yes, you told me that you planned to take a wife,' she said, almost calmly. 'I've known that all along and I should have anticipated that this would happen sooner, rather than later. I don't know what made me react like that.'

But she did know. It was love. Devious and unwanted love—making her behave in a way she didn't like. *If she let it.*

'I should have told you,' he said.

She forced herself to meet his eyes, praying that she could keep her hurt from showing. 'But presumably you didn't, because you realised that it would spell the end of our relationship.'

'Yes.' There was a long pause and now his face bore an expression which was unfamiliar to her. Was it determination? The face of a man who had been born to have every one of his wishes granted? 'You know, this doesn't have to end, Cat.'

For a moment, she thought she might have misheard him. She looked at him in confusion. 'I'm sorry?'

'Nothing needs to change. I can live the life expected of me in Qurhah and still have you here. We could make this work. I know we could.'

She stared at him. 'As your mistress, you mean?'

'Why not?' His voice sounded almost…gentle. 'Men in my position often do—and didn't you tell me right from the start that you weren't interested in a conventional relationship.'

For a moment Catrin felt sick. Yes, she had said that—but never had she guessed that one day it might be used against her as an over-sexed man's selfish form of barter. On shaky legs she walked over to the window and opened it, but the warm evening air brought her little relief. She could feel beads of sweat pinpricking her brow as she stared at the darkened park and the lump in her throat made it seem as if some invisible hand were trying to throttle her.

So this was what happened when you made no demands of a man. When you acted like some kind of human cushion. What else could she expect in return, other than he would expect to walk all over her?

Had he stopped to think that such a suggestion might insult as well as hurt her? No, of course he hadn't. He was thinking about what *he* wanted—and clearly he had no desire to give her up.

But when she stopped to think about it—why *wouldn't* he offer her something like that, when she was prepared to accept so little from him? Why, in loving Murat she had become a woman she barely recognised.

She had given him the sanctuary he'd always craved—peace and respite from his busy life in Qurhah. She had welcomed him into her arms whenever he was here. From the moment he set foot inside the penthouse apartment she was his unconditionally. Up until this moment she'd never bothered him with awkward questions. She had demanded nothing of him. Even the gifts he had showered on her, she had accepted only because it seemed to please him. But she had never been in this for the diamonds or the couture clothes. She had enjoyed living with him and hadn't wanted to rock the boat, and in the process had allowed herself to become like some kind of human sponge.

What had happened to the real Catrin? That strong person who had spent her formative years battling to prevent her little sister from being taken into care? The person who'd shopped for food on her way home from school and watched like a hawk while Rachel pored over her books? She might not have passed many exams herself, but she had plenty of Welsh grit inside her. And maybe now was the time to re-discover some of that grit. To show him that she *wouldn't* be walked all over.

She turned to face him, filled now with a curi-ous sense of calm.

'It may be culturally acceptable for the Sultan to keep a mistress once he's married. For all I know, it might be the norm to keep multiple mistresses in these circumstances. I don't imagine that a man of your stamina would find it difficult to accommo-date more than one woman. But you'll forgive me if I pass on your tempting offer.'

His eyes narrowed. 'Are you being sarcastic?'

'Because you're offering me a bit part in your life? Expecting me to provide smiling sex while you take another woman as your bride? Perish the thought that I should resort to something like that!' She flashed him a sarcastic smile. 'And now, if you'll excuse me, I'm going to pack.'

'To pack?' he echoed blankly.

Her pretend smile slipped. Why the hell was she pretending anyway?

'Yes, to pack,' she said. 'You may be a sultan, but at the moment you're sounding like a spoiled little boy who wants to have his cake and eat it. If you seriously think I'm sharing you with another woman… if you really think I would continue to be your mistress if you married someone else, then I suggest you make an appointment with a psychiatrist at the earliest opportunity.'

She turned and marched out towards the bedroom, clicking on lights as she walked, so that the vast apartment became illuminated with soft pools of golden light. But she was aware that Murat was following her. She could sense his presence behind her, dominating the space around him just as it always did. His words halted her before she'd even had a chance to remember exactly where she'd put the small suitcase, which was the only thing she'd brought with her from Wales.

'I don't want you to go,' he said.

'I'll bet you don't.'

'You aren't facing facts, Cat,' he said. 'I don't have a bride. There is no one I'm intending to marry.'

She turned round, surprised by the look of tension which had tightened his features. 'Not yet.'

'Not yet,' he agreed and his voice hardened as he looked at her. 'And certainly not this weekend.'

'What the hell does that mean?'

'That nothing has really changed. We're talking about the hypothetical. About something which may or may not happen. I don't want you to leave. But. more importantly, I don't want you to leave like this.

In anger. In the darkness of the night with no real place to go.' His black gaze burned into her. 'Isn't what we've shared worth more than that?'

She shook her head. 'There is no alternative.'

'Oh, but there is. If I have to lose you, then can't we at least do it in the spirit of all that has gone before? In passion.' He swallowed and, unexpectedly, the words seemed to burst from him, like a tide. 'The greatest passion I have ever known.'

'No,' she said, trying to ignore the look in his dark eyes. Trying not to be influenced by the caress of his words or the hateful prickle of her body. 'Definitely not.'

'Why not?'

For a moment, she didn't answer. How could she? It was hard to think about anything other than her own stupidity right then. She felt as if a veil had been lifted and suddenly she saw her life with disturbing clarity.

She realised she hadn't been as 'modern' as she'd thought. She hadn't *just* been the Sultan's ideal mistress because, all the time, it seemed she'd secretly been nurturing impossible dreams about him. Her foolish heart had been captured a man who had promised her nothing. She had fallen in love with someone who had always been off-limits. And if she was feeling pain now, then surely she should blame herself, not Murat.

'Why not?' he persisted. 'Can't we just have one last weekend together? Two days to say goodbye to each other...properly? Don't we owe each other that much, Cat?'

She looked at him. At the lips she had kissed a thousand times and the eyes which were blazing with dark fire. Her heart missed a beat. Never again would she see that face alive with passion. Nor feel the warmth of his embrace as he bent his head to kiss her.

Pain flooded through her as she considered her options. She could pack her bag and take a cab to some nearby hotel. Bury her head on some alien pillow and sob her heart out. And then pick herself up and start a new life without him.

But deep down she had no appetite for such drama. Her childhood had been characterised by the slamming of doors and the echo of retreating footsteps, and she had grown to hate such excesses of emotion. She heard one of the clocks chiming out midnight and she thought maybe Murat was right. Maybe ending it like this was all wrong. Shouldn't the closing stages of their affair be conducted with the same clinical detachment which had always defined it—couldn't they end it with some degree of *civility*?

He didn't know she had fallen in love with him and if she flounced out at this time of night, wouldn't that only make it obvious? And that was how Murat would remember her. As sad Cat. Heartbroken Cat. As the woman who had laid her feelings on the line, even though she'd known it was hopeless.

Maybe it was time to show him that she wasn't

some hapless victim. That she had enough resolve and experience not to let *anything* defeat her. She'd grown up fighting against the odds and time after time she'd come through. That was the *real* Cat.

The question was whether she was strong enough to carry it off.

She stared at him. 'One weekend,' she said. 'No more.'

'Cat—'

He stepped towards her but she shook her head, halting him with an almost imperious raise of her hand. 'No, Murat. I'm not in the mood for some passionate make-up sex. Quite frankly, I'm exhausted and I need some space. In fact, I'm going for a long bath and then I'm going straight to sleep. So please don't bother waiting up for me.'

She walked past him and, although her heart was beating like mad, she felt strangely calm. She had done the unthinkable—she had resisted him. She had agreed to his proposal, yes, but he was about to discover that it was going to be on *her* terms.

Still revelling in her brief sense of triumph, she saw the unmistakable look of astonishment on his face.

# CHAPTER FIVE

'I THOUGHT I told you not to wait up for me.'

From his half-reclining position on the bed, Murat glanced up from the papers he'd been working on, to see Cat framed in the doorway of their bedroom. Her dark hair was piled into a thick twist on top of her head and her cheeks were flushed from the long bath she had insisted on taking, leaving him in the unfamiliar position of waiting. A short, towelling robe was knotted tightly around her narrow waist and her legs gave off a silky sheen of newly mois-turised skin. And she still looked angry.

His papers forgotten, he leaned back against the pillows. 'Did you really think that I'd be able to go to sleep after what's just happened?'

She shrugged. 'I have no idea. Your current be-haviour is something of a mystery to me, but that won't be my problem after this weekend is over.'

She walked over to one of the drawers and Murat watched as she pulled out one of the nightgowns she usually only wore whenever they were travelling. There was a brief flash of flesh as the towelling robe was swiftly replaced by the slither of creamy silk and lace as she pulled the gown over her head.

'You don't usually wear anything in bed,' he observed.

She straightened up and looked at him. 'Ah, but these are not usual times, Murat. Even you must realise that.' Pulling the pins from her hair, she went to turn off the light, but he shook his head.

'No. Don't put the light out.'

'It's late.'

'I know what time it is.'

She pulled back the duvet. 'I hate to disappoint you, but I'm still not in the mood for sex.'

'No.' And the strange thing was that neither was he. Oh, he was aroused just from looking at her, that much was a given. He could feel the heavy beat of desire as she climbed into bed beside him. But he recognised that having sex now would somehow be inappropriate, like going out to dinner and discovering you'd forgotten to put your trousers on. Too much had been left unsaid. There was too much distance between them. Her body language was unfamiliarly cool. And it was funny…but when you took sex out of the equation, it forced you to look at a situation with a new and disturbing clarity.

With a start he realised just how much he took her for granted. How he always expected her to be instantly acquiescent whenever he arrived back in London. Always smiling. Always scented. Eagerly opening her arms and her thighs for him. Letting him rip the exquisite lingerie from her body before

ravishing her. Because that was how women had always allowed him to behave. How they *wanted* him
to behave. Indeed, it seemed to feed into the fanta-
sises of most women to discover just how sexually
masterful he could be. He had grown up in a macho
culture where the wishes of men reigned supreme
and he'd certainly never come up against any oppo-
sition to that viewpoint from the opposite sex.

She was the perfect mistress, of course she was,
because she completely sublimated herself to his desires and wishes. Yet while that had always been
immensely satisfactory, wasn't this new and unpre-
dictable Cat making his heart race in an unexpectedly powerful way?

He placed his papers on the bedside table and
turned to look at her. Her eyes were tightly closed
and for a moment he almost smiled at the fierce look
of determination on her face. 'Look at me,' he said.

'I don't want to look at you. I'm still angry with
you.'

'I know you are—and I recognise that you have
a right to be. I should have spoken to you about
what was happening and I think we both know why
I didn't. But we've discussed that and we can't go
back and change it.' His voice lowered. 'And I'm
wondering if we're going to waste our last weekend
together fighting?'

At this, her eyelashes fluttered open, their feath-
ered darkness revealing a vivid emerald gaze which
was tinged with reproach.

'What else did you have in mind instead of fight-

ing? I've just told you that I'm not in the mood for
sex and since that's pretty much your only method of
communication, then I imagine you must be stumped
about what to do next.'

He leaned over her, inhaling the scent of her clean
skin. He felt the unsteady skip of his heart. 'How
about a simple kiss goodnight?'

Catrin stared up into the hawk-like face which
was now inches away from hers. She felt…disori-
entated. As if night had suddenly become day. As if
she had woken from a dream into a new world she
barely recognised. All she knew was that the balance of power between them had shifted and she
was on unfamiliar territory. Suddenly, Murat was
on the back foot. He wasn't demanding from her, or
just reaching out and taking. For once he seemed to
be seeking her permission—even her approval. And
he was about to discover that she wasn't letting him
off that lightly.

She gave him a candid look. 'It won't just be a
goodnight kiss though, will it? You won't be satisfied with that.'

'I may not be satisfied with it,' he said, 'but that
doesn't mean I can't do it.'

Something in his response made her bite back a
reluctant smile and, chastely, she turned her cheek
towards him. 'Oh, very well. One kiss, that's all.'

But gently, he captured her chin between his
thumb and forefinger and slowly turned her head
around to face him. She saw the flicker of something

she didn't recognise in his eyes before he lowered his head towards hers.

It was a butterfly kiss. The faintest brush of his mouth against hers. Such a grazing touch that it was barely there—but it was enough to set her senses on fire. She could feel the warmth of his breath mingling with hers. She could feel the lick of his saliva, as the tip of his tongue flicked tantalisingly at the entrance to her mouth.

And instantly, she wanted him to insert his tongue fully, to mimic the action of a far greater intimacy which her body was already beginning to crave. Her breasts grew heavy and the honeyed ache deep in her belly made her want to wriggle her body against him.

The hands which had been pillowed behind her head now moved automatically to rest on the bunched muscles of his powerful shoulders. Her fingertips began to dig gentle grooves into the silken flesh as he brought her body close to his.

She could feel his arousal pressing hard against her belly and her blood thickened. She wanted to part her thighs for him. She wanted him to touch her where she was aching to be touched, but even though the effort nearly killed her—she forced herself to pull away.

The way he was looking at her was making her feel vulnerable and she felt a flush of colour creeping into her cheeks. Because she hadn't seen that expression of indulgence on his face for a long time. Not since... She swallowed.

Not since the first time she'd met him.

Her heart gave a sudden hard thump. What had happened to that woman who had crisply chided him for his lack of manners? Who had treated him like an equal, even though he'd been a customer and she'd been serving behind the bar. She hadn't known that he was a sultan back then, and she hadn't cared.

She had allowed herself to become intimidated by his power and position, that was what had happened. She had given Murat complete control over her. She had become weak, over-accommodating and completely compliant. Was it any wonder that he'd started to treat her with such a flagrant lack of respect?

With an effort, she pulled away from him, sliding across the cool sheet to the other side of the bed and putting a wide expanse between them. 'A kiss, I said.'

She heard the disbelief in his voice, which he failed to disguise. 'And that's all?'

A wave of power washed over her—so potent, that it was almost worth the aching sense of frustration which was gnawing away at her. 'That's all.' She yawned and then turned her back on him. 'Goodnight, Murat.'

For a moment there was silence until, with what sounded like a small growl, he snapped off the light so that the room was plunged into darkness.

She might have been frustrated, but Catrin felt curiously liberated as she lay there, listening to Murat moving restlessly beside her. And maybe all the see-sawing emotional energy had exhausted her, because her eyelids grew heavy and her body began to relax against the mattress.

When her eyelashes fluttered open, it was to discover that it was morning and that Murat was already awake. He lay propped up on one elbow watching her—his powerful body striped with gold by the shafts of sunlight filtering in through the blinds. Usually, she would have lifted a lazy finger to his lips, or touched his hard, bare torso with a hand which had already begun to tremble with lust. Or leaned forward to kiss him.

But as she had told him last night, this was not usual.

Beneath the duvet, she stretched, aware of the hungry gaze which swept over her, glad he couldn't see the way that her breasts prickled instantly in response.

'Sleep well?' he questioned drily.

'Like a baby. Did you?'

'No.' He gave a hard smile. 'Did you really expect me to, when I had you beside me like some hormonally charged distraction? Allowed to look but not to touch—something I found especially difficult in view of the fact that your goodnight kiss nearly blew me away.'

Remembering the near-innocence of that kiss, Catrin levered herself up the bed a little and looked into the dark gleam of his eyes. 'Then I must thank you for not touching.'

'You're welcome.'

But his curt reply was replaced by a look which came as close to confusion as any she'd ever seen on his face before.

'Do you know,' he mused, 'that's actually the first time I've ever kissed a woman without having sex with her afterwards.'

'And how did it feel?'

'How do you think it felt? How many words in the dictionary are there to describe frustration?' He lay back against the pillows and stared up at the ceiling, thinking about the restless night he'd endured. Yet his restraint had been commendable, hadn't it? At one point she had snuggled up to him, still fast asleep. He'd felt the warmth of her soft flesh as her body had unconsciously invited him to hold her closer, as it had done a hundred times before. And he had found himself unbearably tempted to indulge in that half-asleep sex which always seemed so lazy and decadent.

But he had resisted. As surely as the falcon flew across the desert sands, he had wriggled away from her and spent the next few minutes in a torture of exquisite agony. He had overridden his own desires and told himself that he had no choice. He didn't want Cat waking up to find him making love to her and then accusing him of taking advantage of her. Yet the experience had left him shaken and slightly bewildered, because it wasn't like him to tiptoe around a woman's feelings.

Her soft voice broke into his thoughts.

'What about some coffee?'

Relieved that some kind of normality was returning to a life which seemed to have been turned upside down, he nodded and smiled. 'I'd love some.'

But she was shaking her dark head and she seemed to be having difficulty controlling her laughter. 'That isn't what I meant. I'm not offering. My role as your quasi servant, as the woman who runs around making your life comfortable, is over. I'm preparing us both for the brave new world which lies ahead. So why don't you make the coffee for once?'

For a moment there was silence.

'Me?'

'You,' she agreed.

His eyebrows knitted together. 'Are you serious?'

'Never more so.'

There was another pause during which he was clearly testing her resolve before he got out of bed. Towering over her, seemingly unaware that he was totally naked and very aroused, he held her gaze for a fraction too long before heading off in the direction of the kitchen.

It was a small victory but one which pleased her inordinately, and once he'd gone Catrin took the opportunity to slip into the bathroom, where some of her composure left her. She stared at her face in the mirror. The no-sex of the proceeding night and this morning's role reversal made what was happening seem almost like a dream. But it was not a dream, she reminded herself. It was real.

*And after this weekend, he would be gone from her life for good.*

She hated the fear which iced her skin as she tried to imagine life without Murat. What would fill the great empty space in her life, once her sultan lover was no longer coming home to her?

She felt panic wash over her but she forced herself to push it away, telling herself that she had come through much worse than the end of a love affair. Did she really want to carry on living her life like that—docile and submissive and completely under the thumb?

*Like hell she did.*

Defiantly, she pulled on a pair of jeans and a light, silky shirt and went to find Murat in the kitchen, now dressed and pouring out two cups of delicious-smelling coffee.

It was strange to see him in such an unfamiliar role and she walked over to one of the high stools around the breakfast bar, and sat down.

'Smells good,' she said as he handed her a cup. She took a cautious sip. 'Tastes good, too. It's funny, but I never imagined you adapting to domesticity with so much ease.'

'Didn't you realise that there's no end to my talents?' The glance he shot her was mocking. 'Maybe you should have asked me to make you coffee before.'

Catrin nodded. Maybe she should. 'Although you *have* had servants running around after you all your life, so I wasn't entirely sure you'd be able to cope.'

'I don't think you'd need to be an astrophysicist to be able to decipher the instructions on the side of a packet of coffee,' he commented wryly. 'And I have learnt the art of self-sufficiency in the desert.'

'Really?' She took another sip of coffee.

'Really.' His dark gaze swept over her. 'Even a sultan must know how to fend for himself. I have made meals from roots and brewed pots of sweet tea when I have been setting up camp with my troops. Fundamental lessons of self-sufficiency are essential when preparing for warfare—and all men are equal in the desert.'

Cat heard the sudden hard note of passion which had entered his voice. Had he enjoyed that kind of self-sufficiency and equality? It must have been elusive to someone who had grown up in a palace. But she'd never really given him the chance to do that, had she? With her, he hadn't had to lift a finger. She had taken over every domestic element of their life together as she'd tried so hard to be his textbook lover. And maybe he hadn't wanted her to try that hard. Maybe he had wanted more equality than she'd been prepared to give him. It was a sobering thought.

'The desert sounds…amazing,' she said, aware of how wistful her voice sounded.

'It is,' he agreed. 'Although it is also a barren and unforgiving place, where the instinct for survival takes precedence over everything else.'

The instinct for survival.

Catrin's heart began to pound as she thought about her own survival instinct. Where was that instinct now? Forgotten beneath that undeniably hungry look he was slanting at her, making her wish that things hadn't changed and that she could just go over to him and lose herself in his embrace. She forced herself to focus on the sunlight which was spilling onto the pots of flowers on the terrace outside. 'It's a gorgeous day.'

'I know it is. What do you want to do?'

She knew the answer he wanted. The answer she was longing to give him. She wanted to go straight back to bed, only this time to make love. She wanted his kiss and the hard thrust of his body. She wanted him to take away this ache of desire which was pooling softly at the base of her belly and to rid her of this terrible sense of frustration.

But something told her that would be a cop-out. And right now she felt much too vulnerable to risk having sex with him.

'I'd like to do something different. Something on my terms for once.'

'Such as?'

She looked out at where the rest of the city lay far below them. 'I'd like to go somewhere without you being shadowed by a whole team of bodyguards. I'd like to get in a black cab and go to the cinema and eat popcorn without anyone knowing who you are. I'd like to pretend that we're just the same as any other couple.'

'Anonymity, you mean?'

'That's exactly what I mean.'

He looked at her for a moment and then, brilliantly and unexpectedly, he smiled. 'Then I place myself in your hands completely, Cat,' he said softly.

She felt a warm glow of satisfaction as she finished her coffee and went off to get ready, while Murat spoke quietly to his bodyguards. And although they weren't happy, they agreed to a very low-key presence throughout the day.

For Catrin, it felt like another small triumph. She knew it didn't mean much, but for her it meant a good deal. The hours which lay before them seemed to have endless possibilities. And *she* was the one making all the choices.

They walked across Hyde Park and ate breakfast croissants in a café overlooking the glittering waters of the Serpentine. They walked along the riverbank, before making their way to Covent Garden, where they found a small art gallery which was, inexplicably, almost empty. It felt liberating to walk from painting to painting, discussing each one in detail, and she almost forgot the shadowy presence of the bodyguard hovering discreetly in the next room. She made Murat stand in the queue at the cinema and could tell from his attitude that queuing was an entirely new concept for him. She knew that one word would lead to them being whisked into the grandest seats and generally being fussed over, but Catrin didn't want that. She didn't want anyone to know who he was.

*She wanted him all to herself.*

Afterwards they went to Soho, mingling with crowds of tourists and theatre-goers beneath the gaudy lights. They ate hot slices of pizza and then found a quiet pub in one of backstreets, where they sat quietly drinking cola.

In the taxi home he held her hand, turning it over to study her palm as if he were reading her future. And Catrin felt stupidly choked by the simple gesture, quickly turning her head to look out of the window before he could see how suddenly vulnerable she felt.

'Cat,' he said.

Blinking away the sudden moistness in her eyes, she waited until she had composed herself before she turned to look at him. 'What?'

'Don't ordinary couples usually kiss in taxis?'

She shrugged. 'I have no experience of kissing in taxis.'

'You do now,' he said roughly as his pulled her into his arms.

This was no semi-chaste kiss like the one they'd shared in bed last night. This was lust: pure and potent. Her breathing grew erratic as his finger traced a provocative line over the zip of her jeans and she gasped helplessly into his mouth.

'I want you,' he whispered. 'And if I could, I would have you now. Right here. In the back of this cab. I'd like to pull your wretched jeans down to your ankles and thrust myself deep inside you. I'd like to watch you writhe around on the seat and then I'd like to see you tip your head back and come, while the scent of our sex filled the air. Would you like that, Cat?'

'Stop it,' she whispered, her mouth so dry that she could barely get the words out.

'I don't want to stop it, and neither do you.'

The cab slowed to a halt and Cat was still trembling as they got out and she stood waiting while Murat pulled out his wallet. She remembered him telling her that, unlike many royals, he always carried cash with him because it made him feel slightly ridiculous to have to ask one of his aides for money.

But she frowned when she saw the driver peel off some change and hand it to him and she stepped forward.

'Um. We gave you a fifty-pound note, not a twenty,' she said.

The driver mimed incomprehension, but Cat was nothing if not persistent and she stood her ground and argued the point, until eventually they walked away with the correct change.

'You know, I could have easily afforded to lose thirty pounds,' said Murat wryly as they rode up in the elevator.

'That's not the point,' she said, looping her arms around his neck. 'It's a matter of principle. You shouldn't have to pay more, just because you're rich.'

His lips grazed over hers. 'Quite the little hustler, aren't you?'

'They call it being street-smart,' she said lightly. 'And it's only because I've had to be.'

They shut the door on the bodyguards and turned to each other, but, although the removal of their clothes was fraught with hunger, the sex which followed was different from anything Catrin had known before. For a start, Murat's fingers were trembling as much as hers as he undressed her and for once his smooth dexterity seemed to have deserted him.

He didn't usually frame her face in the palms of his hands and look down at her as if he was only just seeing her properly for the first time.

But she didn't usually have to bite back tears during sex either—aware that her pleasure was heightened by a cruel reality which reminded her that the end of the affair lay just around the corner.

# CHAPTER SIX

THE SEX WAS different.

Actually, Catrin quickly realised that pretty much *everything* was different.

Pressing the *send* button in reply to the text she'd just received from her sister, she walked out onto the terrace, where Murat was busy talking on the phone in the late afternoon sunshine. His Qurhahian aide Bakri often phoned at this time and the two men usually engaged in long talks about state affairs, which completely engrossed him. But today he looked up as he heard her approach and she read the slow smoulder of approval in his eyes.

Her heart lurched. The last day of their last weekend. Two days during which all the normal rules of their relationship seemed to have changed.

Or maybe it was simply her attitude which had changed. She had shown him a stronger Cat. A more decisive Cat. And in response, Murat had become more of an equal and less of a master.

He'd grown more tactile in ways which didn't just involve sex. He held her in his arms when he was watching a football game. He had even cooked her lunch, while she sat on one of the window seats quietly finishing a book she couldn't bear to put down. For two days, at least, their roles had been reversed and it made her wonder how on earth she had been prepared to accept so little from him before.

But she had set the agenda, hadn't she? Murat had simply followed it. What man in the world wouldn't lie back and enjoy a woman running round after him like that?

Inevitably, she found herself wishing that she could stay. She told herself that nothing was stopping her from doing that, since Murat had told her over and over that he didn't want her to leave. Until she forced herself to remember that they still had no future together. All he was offering was a role as his mistress—and who knew when somebody younger and prettier would come along and supplant her? Because that was what happened to mistresses. Easy come, easy go.

She had the kind of background which most men would shy away from—let alone a powerful sultan. She was still the illegitimate daughter of an alcoholic mother and nothing would ever change *that*, either.

She thought back to the text she had just received from Rachel.

*Really worried about Mum.*

Catrin had felt fear descend on her like a dark cloud. She'd done all the stuff that the counsellors always recommended. In a hurried phone call, made while Murat had been in the shower, she had reminded her sister that she needed to take a step back. That nobody could stop an alcoholic from drinking if they were determined to do so. She didn't want Rachel wasting any more of her university vacation, trying to help someone who didn't want to be helped. She told her that next week she would be travelling down to Wales and she would take over and sort it out...though she wasn't quite sure how. It was not a prospect she was looking forward to, but some strange kind of loyalty made it impossible to walk away from the mess her mother had made of her life.

And in the meantime, she still had the bitter task of saying goodbye to Murat.

The light summer breeze on the terrace was ruffling his black hair as he clicked off his phone and looked at her and she thought that he had never looked quite as gorgeous or as accessible as he did in that moment.

'Such a serious expression,' he mused. 'You're not regretting your decision to leave, are you?'

She said the words with way more conviction than she felt. 'Definitely not.'

'Are you sure?' he persisted. 'You don't sound very sure. Think how good it's been these last couple of days, Cat. And then think about all the days we could have together in the future.'

She was tempted. Of course she was. Faced with the choice of going it alone, or staying here with the man she still loved, there wasn't much of a contest. *Except that this wasn't real.* She was only ever going to be a stopgap in Murat's life—and that was no longer enough.

She shrugged. 'I have no doubt it would be wonderful in lots of ways, but it isn't going to happen. So I'd advise you not to waste your time by trying to change my mind.'

His black gaze flicked over her, making her skin tingle as if someone had just brushed it with fire.

'But what about if I asked for an extension?'

She narrowed her eyes at him. 'What kind of extension?'

He leaned back against the wrought-iron balustrade and continued to study her, his attention lingering on the thrust of her breasts which were pushing insistently against her silky white shirt. 'You remember I planned to meet with the wind-farm consortium in Italy?'

'I thought that was next month.'

'It was. But what if I'd managed to bring it forward? What if I told you that I'd persuaded Niccolo and Alekto to juggle their schedules and that we're all flying out to Umbria tomorrow? Would you come with me, Cat?'

'You're telling me that you've managed to get two such powerful men to change their busy schedules based on nothing more than one of your whims?'

'No, not on one of my whims.' His mouth hardened into an implacable line. 'More a determination to hang onto you for as long as possible.'

She shook her head. 'You only want me because

time is running out and because you're used to getting your own way.'

'No,' he negated, and suddenly his voice sounded harsh and almost rough. 'I want you because in all the time I've known you, I've never stopped wanting you and I don't think I ever will.'

'Murat—'

'But even putting aside your undoubted allure, your skill at playing hostess on these occasions has never been in any doubt. You make business seem almost like fun, and people always relax more if there is a woman around.' He paused. 'Two more days, that's all. Think about it. Two days in the Italian sun with nothing to think about other than topping up your tan. Surely that must tempt you into changing your mind?'

Catrin gave a flat laugh. *Topping up her tan?* Didn't he have any idea of what was going on inside her head? About her silent struggle to imagine the future, when she left this gilded world of his?

'Stop being so manipulative.'

'But sometimes manipulation is the only thing which works,' he said, pulling her into his arms and tightening his hold on her waist before she had the chance to object.

His touch weakened her defences and the slow brush of his lips over hers made her want to melt. Yes, the sex was *very* different, she thought as he slipped his hand inside her bra. He made it feel as if it *meant* something. And it didn't. It was still just sex.

But she made no protest as he led her back inside

the apartment and started undressing her. And she let him. She did more than just let him. She assisted him. She helped him pull open her clothes with hands which were shaking almost as much as hers were, as her mouth reached hungrily for his.

She groaned as he touched her. And she writhed as he traced a finger around where she was hot and moist and quivering for his touch. Impatiently, he ripped open her panties and she took him into her arms, her eyes closing helplessly as she felt his warm weight on top of her. Did the sex just feel more poignant because the clock was ticking? she wondered. And was it the same for him?

She saw the flash of something unfamiliar in his eyes as he entered her with one slick stroke, before quickly finding his rhythm. He spoke in his native tongue as he moved—strange, guttural words which filled her with a terrible *sadness*, even while her orgasm began to build. Her body clenched just as he cried out her name, and her arms tightened around his back as pleasure swept over her.

Catrin could feel the dying spasms as he emptied his seed inside her—and all she could think was that some day his seed would bear fruit. But not with her. Some other woman would carry his child, but it would never be her.

He stirred and stroked an errant spill of hair away from her flushed face, levering himself up onto his elbows to stare down at her. 'What would you say if I told you that today was one of the best days of my life? As was yesterday, and the day before that.'

'I'd say you were being too smooth for your own good.'

He smiled, pulling her closer and burying his mouth in her hair. 'Come to Italy with me, Cat,' he said. 'One last trip abroad, together. That's all.'

'I can't.'

'Why not?'

'You know why not. Because it's a bad idea.' Half-heartedly, she tried to disentangle herself from his arms. 'And will you please stop looking at me with that little-boy look? Because it isn't going to work.'

'Cat.'

He even made saying her name sound erotic and she could feel her resolve slipping. And suddenly she felt too overwhelmed with conflicting emotions and lingering pleasure to be able to resist him any longer. And why keep resisting something she really wanted to do?

'A few days,' she said. 'That's all. And after that I'm leaving.'

His eyes glittered as he stroked his hand over her bottom. 'Of course you are.'

# CHAPTER SEVEN

THE ITALIAN COUNTRYSIDE was beautiful in a take-your-breath-away kind of way but Murat barely noticed the lush green hills swathed with silvery olive trees, or the distant glimmer of the lake. Instead, his attention was focused on the woman beside him and a deep sense of feeling thwarted filled him, as his powerful cavalcade of cars moved through the Italian countryside.

With her mahogany hair gleaming and her body perfectly still, she wasn't behaving as he'd expected her to behave. As he *wanted* her to behave—especially now that she had finally given in to his desire that she accompany him to Umbria.

During the flight from London she had kept him at a distance. In every way. She had been polite, yes. Each comment he'd made had been answered with a studied courteousness, although he noticed that she had initiated no conversation of her own. She had picked up a book and started to read and although the book had now been put away in her handbag, it made no difference. He didn't like being ignored by a woman—especially not one who had previously been so attentive. Who had behaved like a wildcat that last time they had made love...

With her hands lying clasped on her lap and her simple blue dress seeming to echo her muted mood, he couldn't remember her ever looking quite so serene, nor so beautiful.

Tightly, his hands clenched into fists where they lay on top of his tensed thighs. Was it because the end was in sight that he found himself wanting her more than ever? Or had her own accusation contained more than a kernel of truth? Was it a case of his competitive nature governing him as it had always governed him—driven by the knowledge that he was rarely refused anything, by anyone?

Yet deep down he recognised that it wasn't quite that simple. The woman she had become since she'd discovered his secret courtship had been like the Cat he'd fallen for. The feisty beauty who had blown him away within seconds of meeting her. Who had looked at the powerful potentate standing in that humble Welsh hotel and spoken to him as if he were...

An equal?

Maybe.

This past weekend, she had been like a butterfly fluttering in out of the sunshine in order to be admired and yet somehow managing to remain tantalisingly aloof. Suddenly, everything had been on *her* terms. She had kept him guessing. Waiting. She had made him feel uncertain in a way which was totally new to him. And in the time it had taken before she had finally let him back into her arms, he had felt as if he were going out of his mind.

He shook his head in consternation, for he was not given to self-analysis. From childhood, he had been taught to be ruthless and strong. He had been told that his role was to protect and to provide for his country; to sublimate his own desires in the pursuit of those goals. It had been drummed into him that his destiny was to rule with resilience and never appear vulnerable. And that had been the maxim he had embraced all his life.

He had seen less war than his father, mainly because he didn't share the dead king's unquenchable lust to conquer new territories, and because he had preferred to use the intricate skills of international diplomacy rather than force. But Murat had seen his own fair share of battle. Etched into his memory was that terrible clash with insurgents at Port D'Leo, when his two most senior commanders had been slain before his eyes. He remembered holding the hand of one of the men, as his lifeblood had seeped like liquid rust into the hot, desert sand. He remembered the choked words which the soldier had asked Murat to take back to his wife: words of regret that he would not live to see his unborn child. And Murat could still recall his own guilt that he had been powerless to save them.

He thought back to his spartan childhood. Of the loneliness of his life in the palace and of the powerful father who had never been there for him, nor for any of his family. Any snatched hours spent with his son had been spent teaching him weaponry and horsemanship, and drumming into him that women could weaken a man and sap his essential strength.

But Murat could never remember being shown affection by the man who had sired him. Even his mother's love had been diluted by her long, depressive illness, when she would sit staring at the blank wall of her sitting room, rather than engaging with Murat or his sister.

And wasn't that the truth about human emotion—that you could never rely on it? He thought of his friend Suleiman, the person to whom he had once been closer than to anyone in the world, and the man Murat had relied upon to give his sovereign one hundred per cent unswerving loyalty.

Yet Suleiman had let the wiles of a woman twist him away from that loyalty and devotion, hadn't he? He had taken the woman destined to be Murat's bride and had made her his own. And although Murat had now forgiven his oldest friend, he still felt the bitter twist of pain when he remembered how his blood brother had betrayed him.

And that was why he had always kept his heart steeled against an emotion which some men called love, but which Murat saw as nothing but trouble. Human hearts could not be trusted, nor relied upon—and 'love' was the most unreliable emotion of all. Far better to stay clear of the clutches of something which had the power to destroy much of what it touched.

'Hadn't you better tell me about this meeting?'

Catrin said, her voice breaking his thoughts as she crossed one leg over the other.

It was difficult to concentrate on anything other than the toned gleam of her ankles, but Murat did his best. 'Well, Niccolo you have, of course, already met.'

'Yes.' There was a pause. 'And is he bringing the lovely Lise with him?'

'He didn't say.' His gaze slid over her. 'Will you have a problem with that, if he does?'

She shrugged. 'It's not my place to have a problem with it. And anyway, she was only telling the truth. If it hadn't been for Lise, I might still be stumbling around in the dark. Maybe I should be grateful to her, for making me face up to the truth and to see our relationship for what it really is…*was*,' she corrected hastily. 'Who else is coming?'

'Alekto Sarantos,' he said. 'We met him once in Paris, if you remember?'

Memory was a road Catrin didn't want to take, but sometimes someone planted you on that super-fast highway and there wasn't a thing you could do about it. She recalled a man with ebony hair and extraordinary blue eyes. Alekto had been surrounded by women, looking more like a rock star than a businessman. But he had seemed almost bored by the adoration of the women surrounding him, as if he would rather be anywhere else than at the city's most glitzy party.

Unlike her, who had been revelling in every glorious moment. It had been like a dream come true. The most romantic city in the world. With Murat.

Her heart gave a painful wrench as she remembered tickertape cascading from the ceiling at midnight, and the Sultan laughing as he brushed the streams of paper from her face, before bending his head to kiss her.

'I remember,' she said, swallowing down the lump in her throat.

She bent her head to stare at her hands, because anything was better than having to look into his hard, hawk-like face and meet the black gleam of his eyes. Every time she looked at him she wanted to touch him. And every time she touched him, it would just make their inevitable parting all the harder. That was a certainty which had been growing all day.

She had realised her mistake in agreeing to come here from the moment she'd stepped onto the plane, discovering that it was all too easy to slip back into the role of being Murat's consort. It had suddenly dawned on her that she needed to put some kind of distance between the two of them in order to protect herself, which was why she had pulled back a little during the flight. But it hadn't been easy to remain neutral—not when the Sultan was behaving with such attentiveness towards her.

'Look up there,' he said suddenly. 'We are approaching the Gardinello estate.'

She looked out of the window to where an elaborate pair of wrought-iron gates was opening to let them through. Their car moved slowly up a steep incline, before coming to a halt outside an ochre-tinted farmhouse. Catrin stepped out into a sunny courtyard filled with pots of tumbling white flowers, where a cat lay sleeping peacefully beneath the shade of an olive tree. Tiered gardens were planted with cypress and cherry trees and she breathed in the heady scent of sun-warmed herbs, and flowers.

'Look behind you,' said Murat softly.

She turned round to see olive groves and vineyards and a sprawling orchard of fruit trees. There was the glimmer of an infinity pool and, beyond that, the mirrored expanse of Lake Trasimeno. Suddenly, she found herself filled with a powerful sense of yearning, fuelled by the beauty of her surroundings and by the strength of her feelings for the man who stood beside her.

Sliding on her sunglasses, she tried desperately to regain some of her lost equilibrium—trying to focus on the mundane rather than the impossible. Everywhere she looked she could see activity. Their cases were being removed from the car by people whose names she would probably never know and inside the house there would be yet more people preparing food and ensuring that all the Sultan's needs would be met. Bodyguards were moving swiftly towards the forested area which bordered the top of the estate, presumably to check that the fences were secure. She saw them muttering into their cell phones as they scaled the green bank. With something of a shock, she realised she'd grown used to this life of being guarded and protected—and in a funny kind of way she was even going to miss *that*.

'Where are the others?' she asked.

'They're arriving later.'

Her eyes met his. 'How much later?'

'Does it matter? I want some more time alone with you, Cat. And ultimately, I want you to change your mind about leaving me.'

'That isn't going to happen.' She bit her lip. 'And you're not making this very easy for me.'

'That was never my intention.' His black eyes gleamed. 'Did you really think it would be?'

She gave a short laugh. Of course she hadn't. She'd watched him enough in the past during count-less dinners with business colleagues, when he'd been at his manipulative best. Murat would always use whatever method was best suited to make sure he always got exactly what he wanted. 'No. If I'd stopped to think about it, I should have guessed that you would do exactly this.'

'So why not just relax and try to accept it? Come and I'll show you around, and let's see if the beauty of the Italian countryside won't wipe some of that tension from your face.'

Her palms felt clammy and her head felt light as she realised he was doing that thing he did so well. That dominant, masterful thing which made her just want to…to what? To go back to being the compli-ant person she'd been before—the one he'd used to leave at home like an ornament, while he'd courted his royal princess?

But she followed him along the gravelled paths which interweaved the different levels of the gardens, because what else was she going to do? Her canvas sneakers sank into the dusty summer grass and the warm sunshine seeped into her skin. And even though she'd started out by feeling completely strung out, it was perhaps inevitable that some of the tension would leave.

It felt peculiar to be walking alongside him like this—the future forgotten, while they enjoyed the beauty of the Italian gardens. The sunlight glinted off his hair and from time to time she glanced up at him, forcing herself to walk just far enough away to avoid touching him.

She was relieved when they arrived back at the main farmhouse, though less so when he showed her into a cool and shuttered room which commanded a spectacular view over the distant hills. She stared at the amazing view outside, because anywhere was better than glancing at the huge bed which dominated the room.

Murat shut the door and the walls seemed to close in on her as he came towards her, with that dark look of lust which was so achingly familiar.

'I want you, Cat,' he said. 'I want you so badly that I can hardly think straight.'

And she wanted him, too.

She wanted him in a way which made her heart burn and her body ache. She wanted to let him blot out every nagging thought and fear with his kiss. But she couldn't. She couldn't pretend—not any more.

If he made love to her now, then wouldn't she be in danger of blurting out how much she loved him—making herself even more vulnerable in the process?

She'd been guilty of playing a part when she lived with him and if she wasn't careful she was going to find herself doing the same thing again. Oh, it might be a different part, but it would still involve hiding the real Catrin.

Because how could she continue to have sex with him and yet behave as if nothing had changed? As if fleeting pleasure had the power to blot out the dark reality of losing him. Wasn't it likely that the more she gave to him, the emptier it would leave her?

She stared at his hard, warrior's face and his hard, warrior's body. Murat was a hard man, through and through. *He* wouldn't be weeping into his pillow when their affair ended. Oh, he might experience a brief pang of regret and maybe even a few moments of nostalgia, but then he would get on with his life. His powerful life as Sultan, in which there had never been room for a second-rate commoner like her.

'I can't do it, Murat,' she said quietly. 'Not any more.'

'What are you talking about?'

She took a step back, terrified that she would be swayed by his proximity. Afraid that if he remained within touching distance then she might just ignore the voice of reason which was demanding to be heard, and instead crawl into his arms, like a small animal seeking sanctuary.

She met his eyes. 'I can't have sex with you any

more. I thought I could just carry on the way we were, until it was time for me to leave, but I was wrong. I can't.'

'But what has happened to make you act this way?' he demanded. 'We made love in London just before we came here—so what the hell has changed during a two-hour flight?'

She licked her lips, knowing that she couldn't keep hiding her emotions away. That if she wanted him to understand, then she was going to have to *tell* him how she was feeling.

'I have,' she said. 'I've changed. And I've realised that it hurts too much to know we're living on borrowed time. Every kiss we share is like a protracted goodbye. Every time you touch me, it makes me feel…diminished.'

'*Diminished?*'

She saw his eyes narrow and guessed he would be filing her words away under *psychobabble*. But that didn't matter. She no longer had to impress him or try to be his perfect woman. All she had to do was to remain true to herself.

'Yes, diminished.'

He was shaking his dark head. 'I don't understand you, Cat,' he bit out, his voice filled with frustration.

'And you don't need to. When we leave here we won't ever have to see each another again. My role in your life is over. I shouldn't…' For a moment, she stopped. Was that why people hid behind lies so often, because the truth was too painful to confront? 'I shouldn't have agreed to come, but since I have

I'll do what's expected of me. I'll play your perfect hostess one more time—but I can't be intimate with you again. From now on, this relationship has to be platonic. It...*hurts* too much to be anything but platonic. So if you'll excuse me, I'm going to unpack and then shower. I need to get ready for when your guests arrive.'

# CHAPTER EIGHT

BENEATH A JASMINE-COVERED pergola, the long table was laid with heavy silver and crystal, which gleamed golden in the candlelight. Desperately trying to concentrate on the beauty which surrounded her, Catrin sipped from her glass of water. Overhead, bright stars glittered—and occasionally one would shoot through the indigo sky in a blurred silvery trail so fast that if you blinked you would miss it. They had eaten tiny cheese soufflés followed by giant prawns and now they were lingering over the peach sorbet, which a young Italian woman had just served to them.

She sat back and listened to the discussion which was currently taking place between the three men, but in truth she wasn't really paying much attention to the subject of wind farms.

It hadn't been the easiest of days, but she didn't think even Murat would deny that it had been a successful one. They had greeted their guests as a united couple. Somehow they had managed to disguise the brooding tension which had sprung up, following that heated confrontation in the bedroom earlier.

Alekto Sarantos had come by private jet from the Greek island of Santorini, and was accompanied by a sinewy redhead called Suzy, who was clinging to his arm as if she couldn't bear to let him go. Catrin thought she could understand why, since the Greek billionaire was as gorgeous as she remembered from Paris.

He and Suzy had gone straight to their room, emerging several hours later all bright-eyed and laughing softly. As a demonstration of easy sexuality it couldn't have been more apparent, and Catrin knew she hadn't imagined Murat's stony expression as he'd shot a meaningful glance in her direction.

Niccolo arrived alone. He'd flown straight from New York and seemed rather distracted throughout the day. But at dinner, Catrin found herself sitting next to him and found him entertaining company. He told her about meeting Murat on the ski slopes a decade earlier and then talked about growing up in Milan. But as the coffee was being served, he lowered his voice so that only she could hear.

'Listen, I want to apologise for Lise's behaviour towards you the other night.'

Catrin remembered his girlfriend's words puncturing her foolish little world of make-believe and she shook her head. 'Honestly. It's fine, Niccolo. You could have brought her with you, if you'd wanted. I wouldn't have minded.'

'But I would've minded,' he said stubbornly. 'I

don't like women who take pleasure from other people's misfortune.'

Catrin's smile didn't slip, even though she thought his words made her sound like some kind of victim.

*So don't be one.*

'Actually, I think maybe she did me a favour,' she said. 'Sometimes, I think it's best to get things out in the open, don't you?'

But the Italian's expression remained impenetrable as he shook his head. 'On the contrary,' he said. 'In my country secrets are as much a part of us as the air we take into our lungs.' His eyes were curious as he looked from her to Murat, who was sitting on the far side of the table. 'But you have obviously forgiven him.'

Catrin stared down at the melting puddle of peach sorbet in her dish. She knew that Niccolo and Murat went back a long way but even so it would be an unthinkable breach of etiquette to start discussing the Sultan's personal life, no matter how close their friendship. 'It isn't for me to forgive someone like Murat. He is his own master.' She glanced up to see the Italian girl approaching with a tray of coffee and quickly changed the subject. 'Mmm. Doesn't that coffee smell delicious?'

She could hear Suzy giggling at something Murat had said and as she sipped from her dinky cup of espresso, Catrin marvelled at how much she had learnt during her time as the Sultan's consort. She now knew the basics of royal protocol and how to eat an oyster. She could talk knowledgeably about the French Impressionists and was completely at ease around servants and bodyguards. She thought about the life she had come from and the one which lay ahead. And wondered if she would ever eat in a setting as beautiful as this again, with men who owned oil wells or who prowled the fleshpots of the world, with their restless blue eyes.

'What do you think, Cat?'

Murat voice broke into her thoughts and she looked across the table to find his gaze fixed on her. 'Sorry,' she said. 'I was miles away.'

His eyes gleamed in the candlelight. 'Alekto and I are just musing about why the public hate wind farms so much.'

Catrin put her cup down. 'Because they look so startling, I guess.'

'And people don't like that look?' questioned Alekto, swirling wine around in his glass.

'Not really. I think it takes time for them to accept something which is so alien to them—something which looks as if it's come from another planet,' she answered slowly. 'If I wanted to improve the image of wind farms, I'd go to an art college and ask some of the most promising students to create images to make them seem interesting, and then I'd mount an exhibition of their work and create a lot of press interest.  Wind farms as art.  A positive image, for once.'

Niccolo leaned back in his chair. 'That is actually a very good idea. And so brilliantly simple.'

They were all looking at her now, but it was only Murat's face she could see.

'And this,' he said softly, his eyes not leaving her face, 'from the woman who'd never even seen a flowering cactus.'

His words made no sense to anyone else but her, but they made Catrin's heart give a kick of unbearable pain. Why was he reminding her of a time when she hadn't thought beyond the way he had made her feel? She wondered if she would have walked so blindly into the affair if she'd known what awaited her? Of course she wouldn't. Because who, other than a masochistic fool, would open their arms to inevitable heartbreak?

Feeling suddenly claustrophobic, she rose to her feet, forcing herself to smile at them. 'And now I wonder if you'd mind excusing me? I'm going to turn in…it's been a very long day.'

It was indeed late and there was no objection from Niccolo or Alekto—and Suzy was so busy gazing at her Greek lover that she scarcely seemed to hear her. But Murat made no attempt to hide the flash of annoyance which hardened his lips. She knew that going to bed was a cop-out and that maybe she wasn't fulfilling her part of the bargain, but suddenly Catrin didn't care. She couldn't keep pretending that everything was fine. Sitting there with that cool hostess smile on her lips and talking about wind farms, while inside her heart was breaking.

Why the hell had she agreed to come here?

Quickly, she walked towards the house and

slipped into the room she was sharing with Murat without bothering to turn on the light. She could see her phone flashing from inside her handbag and when she pulled it out, she saw that her sister had left two texts.

*Mum on real bender this time,* read the first.

The second was more direct. And of more immediate concern. *Can u come home Cat? Your turn now.*

Guilt rushed through her as she stared at the illuminated screen, realising that she'd barely given a thought to the situation back home. She had been so preoccupied with her own problems that she hadn't stopped to consider Rachel and how she was coping with their drunken mother. And that wasn't *fair.*

The bedroom door opened and the light which flooded in highlighted the powerful figure who was standing in the doorway.

'All alone in the darkness, Cat?' came his soft taunt. He switched on the light. 'Why's that?'

For a moment she didn't answer; she was too busy blinking as her eyes accustomed themselves to the sudden brightness. Shoving her phone down into the bottom of her handbag, she shrugged.

'I'm all for saving on electricity costs,' she said carelessly. 'I thought you'd approve—after all, you're the man who's ploughing his money into wind farms and researching different sources of alternative energy.'

'Very funny. Why did you leave the dinner so abruptly?'

'Because…because I suddenly realised I was

crazy to agree to come here and…' Her words tailed off as she thought about her sister's texts. Maybe she should tell him that she needed to go back to Wales and maybe she should tell him why. And yet… She bit down hard on her bottom lip. How could she bring herself to tell him something like that when they were on the verge of parting for ever? Did she want to be forever remembered as the daughter of a drunk? She felt a flicker of stubborn pride. Her mother's illness was none of Murat's business. She met his eyes. 'And I'd like to go back to England as soon as possible.'

His face hardened.

'Is this your way of playing games?' he demanded. 'Of demonstrating how much power you have over me, by seeing how far you can push me?'

'Of course it isn't.'

'I thought we'd agreed that you were going to stay for a couple of days.'

She stared down at the floor, unwilling to meet the angry gleam in his eyes. 'Maybe I've changed my mind.'

'Oh, really?' His voice was silky. 'Then maybe I should see if I can change it back for you again.'

She should have realised exactly what method he would use and if she'd been thinking straight, she might have given herself time to psych herself up and remain immune to him. But she wasn't thinking straight and therefore she had no defence when Murat reached out and pulled her into his arms.

Instinct took over. She could feel every hard sinew

of his body as she melted against him. And the star-
tled breath she sucked in did her no favours, because
it left her completely accessible to the urgent pressure
of his lips as he bent his head to kiss her.

Her hands went up to his shoulders to push him
away, but as he deepened the kiss she felt herself
clinging on—and then some.

'Murat,' she groaned as he began to ruck up her
dress, his hands skating beneath the delicate fabric
to smooth themselves over her thighs.

But he didn't seem to be listening to her half-
hearted protest; he was too busy tugging her panties
down. The delicate scrap of lace fluttered to the floor
as he carried her over to the bed and laid her down
on it. His thumb was on her clitoris and the gasp-
ing little groan she made in response was quickly
silenced by another kiss.

Her desire was spiralling out of control and as he
pulled away from her she heard the unsteady rasp of
a zip. In the throes of something which felt so wrong
and yet so irresistibly good, her lashes fluttered open
to see Murat kicking off his trousers. His arousal was
heart-stoppingly evident and the fierce look of hunger on his face made her grow weaker still.

And then he was positioning himself over her—
on her and in her—thrusting into her so deeply that
she opened her mouth to scream with pleasure. But
he anticipated her cry and drowned it with another
kiss.

It was a frantic, wordless coupling—one in which
they couldn't seem to get enough of each other. She

had never known Murat quite so out of control before. He bit at her breasts and she bit him back and her orgasm seemed to be torn from some deep, dark place inside her. It ripped her open and left her breathless and dazed. More dazed than she had ever been. Because she knew this was the last time?

She closed her eyes as he jerked violently against her, muttering something soft and indistinct in his native tongue, and Catrin could feel the salty prick of tears at the backs of her eyes as his body grew still at last.

For a moment, neither of them said anything and then his hand tightened at her waist. 'Cat?'

Keeping her eyes tightly closed, she said nothing. There was nothing *to* say. She didn't know what she expected next, but it was not to hear the sound of slow and rhythmic breathing.

Cautiously, she turned her head to look at him.

He was asleep!

The callous brute had fallen asleep!

Anger and indignation flooded through her. How could he go to sleep after what had just happened? Something she had *let* happen. After everything she'd vowed not to do, it seemed she was as weak as a kitten when it came to resisting him.

And now what?

Was she expected to lie here and go to sleep, too? To trot down to breakfast in the morning and face those people as if nothing had happened?

She couldn't.

She ran the tip of her tongue over bone-dry lips.

It seemed that, despite all the experience she had gained, she was still capable of being completely naïve and *stupid*. Or had she really imagined that intimacy wasn't going to happen with a man as virile as Murat? A man she still loved and wanted, no matter how much she told herself it was wrong.

Because as always Murat was in charge. Everything he touched, he controlled—even here, in a house he did not own. He was still calling the shots, wasn't he? Just as he always did. Having sex with her even though she'd told him she didn't want it.

*But you did want it, didn't you?*

And if she stayed here, it was only going to happen again. She would keep making the same mistakes, over and over.

Cautiously she rolled away from him, but he didn't stir and she forced herself to lie there until she could hear the sound of the other guests going to bed—the sounds of their goodnights echoing through the silence.

She lay there until the hand of her watch crept around to two o'clock and the house was completely still, and then she slipped from the bed, tiptoeing across the room to switch the light off. Murat stirred a little, but he did not wake.

Under the cover of darkness, she felt more secure. She crept over to the wardrobe and fished out a clean pair of panties and then put on a pair of cotton trousers beneath her dress. Wrapping a soft pashmina around her neck, she walked quietly over to the desk where Murat had left the official paraphernalia which accompanied him everywhere.

With fingers which were miraculously steady, she found his wallet. The amount of Euros inside was substantial, but she needed enough to pay for a taxi to the airport and a one-way ticket on a commercial airline. So she didn't feel a flicker of guilt as she extracted a wad of notes.

Sliding her feet into her canvas shoes, she picked up her handbag and crept from the bedroom. Through the silent house she moved, using the back door of the kitchen to gain access to the grounds.

Beneath the starry skies, all was quiet and she thanked heaven that there were no guard dogs patrolling the premises. But her heart was still thundering with anxiety as she slipped among the shadows to the boundaries of the property, terrified that one of the bodyguards might hear her.

Among neat rows of broad beans and tomato plants, she found an unlocked gate—presumably one used by the gardener—and she let herself out. Her breathing was laboured as she descended the dusty track they'd driven up earlier. In the distance, she could hear a faint grunting sound and then a rustle. She wondered if that was the sound of wild boar, scrabbling around in the forested area, then told herself not to let her imagination run away with itself. Because rural Italy wasn't so different from rural Wales, was it? She had grown up in the countryside and knew there was little to fear as long as you were sensible.

But nothing had prepared her for a such a night-time journey, in a strange country whose language she did not speak. She experienced a couple of moments of panic, before reminding herself that she had spent her life being adaptable. She was good at it. And how difficult could it be? She could see the small, hilltop glitter of lights in the distance. Lights meant a village and that village must have a taxi.

She had a smartphone with a bilingual dictionary and plenty of money. Even if she couldn't find a cab until morning, it was a warm night and she was perfectly prepared to wait.

All she knew was that she was going to do this—and she was going to do it on her own.

She could be strong and she *would* be strong.

She was going to need to be.

# CHAPTER NINE

THE LOUD POUNDING inside her head wouldn't seem to stop and Catrin raised her fingertips to her throbbing temples and groaned. Her mouth felt bone-dry and her skin was burning up—so why were her teeth chattering as wildly as if she'd been camping out all night on some Arctic waste?

Rolling over on the narrow bed, she picked up her wristwatch and tried to focus on it as the pounding miraculously stopped. She swallowed. Should she take another couple of aspirin to try to bring her temperature down? Was it four hours since she'd had the last lot?

The incessant noise resumed and she realised that it wasn't coming from inside her head, but from outside her door.

'Go away,' she mumbled.

But if whoever was knocking had heard her, they certainly weren't taking any notice. She wondered if she could get away with ignoring the summons, but, whoever it was, they were persistent. It was almost as if somebody knew she was in there and wasn't going

to give up until she answered. Probably someone
who wanted to borrow milk. Or maybe just someone who was lonely and fancied a chat. The place
was full of people like that. Staff accommodation
in hotels like this seemed to be teeming with people
who had sad stories to tell. She had one of her own,
but she suspected that nobody would ever believe it.

Wearily, she got up off the bed and walked over
to the door with something like a smile pinned to her
face. She would say she was ill and hopefully they
would take the hint and beat a hasty retreat.

But her smile faded the moment she pulled the
door open, and her overheated body grew completely still. She blinked once or twice, as if her vision had become faulty, but she quickly realised that
it hadn't. That the most feared and most longed-for
outcome had materialised and Murat was standing
in *her* doorway, looking completely out of place in
his expensive Italian suit, with his black eyes boring into her.

A wave of dizziness washed over her—a mixture of lust and fever and sheer apprehension. She
thought about shutting the door in his face to avoid
a confrontation she didn't want. But what would be
the point? You didn't shut the door on the Sultan of
Qurhah because he would probably use his royal
privilege to get the owner of the hotel to come and
open it for him. Or kick it down himself, most probably. And besides, wouldn't that be a cowardly gesture? She wasn't afraid of Murat and what he had to
say, was she?

Was she?

She ran the back of her hand over her damp brow.

No. She wasn't.

It had taken guts to run away and leave him in the dead of night in that remote part of Italy, and to sit alone in that bus shelter until the small village had woken up and she'd persuaded a taxi to take her to Rome airport. And even more guts to throw her phone away once she'd arrived back in England and Murat had rung her, furiously demanding to know what had happened. She had reassured him that she was safe but she had realised that, as long as he had her number, there would always be the chance that he might contact her. *And the chance that she might be weak enough to go back to him.*

But it seemed he had found her anyway—and it would only play into his hands if she showed him she was scared. Why be scared when he was on *her* territory? All she had to do was concentrate. To remind herself that he was no good for her. She had played out this scene in her head many times, imagining what she'd do if she ever saw him again—and she knew that the most important thing of all was to *act as if she didn't care.*

'Murat,' she croaked.

There was a short silence as he stared at her and, although he seemed to be swimming in and out of focus, the shock on his face was almost palpable. Did she look that bad? She supposed she did. She hadn't washed her hair in days and she couldn't remember the last time she'd eaten. Her jeans felt looser than they used to and her T-shirt was crumpled and creased.

'You're sick!' he accused, as if she'd done something wrong.

'No. I'm fine.' It was unfortunate that she chose just that moment to produce another of those horrible, hacking coughs.

Black eyes raked over her. 'You don't look fine to me. Or sound it.'

'That's none…' She coughed again, putting her hand over her mouth, which made her words come out all muffled. 'None of your business.'

There was a brief silence while Murat noted her flushed cheeks and dull eyes and he felt a sharp pang of something he didn't recognise. He hadn't seen her for weeks. Not since she'd left him in Italy and he'd woken up and reached for her and found the other side of the bed empty. And hadn't he completely lost it at that moment? Hadn't he run outside and threatened to sack every one of his bodyguards for failing to hear her leave? He had been beside himself with worry and fear until word had reached him that somehow she had managed to get herself to Rome airport, where she'd caught a scheduled flight back to London.

And now she was standing in front of him and nothing was how he'd thought it would be. Had he thought her face would light up when she saw him again? That she'd admit that running out on him had been the biggest mistake she'd ever made?

Because if that was the case, he had been badly wrong.

She was staring at him suspiciously—the way an animal did when it was backed into a corner—and she looked terrible. Her hair was plastered to the side of her hot cheeks and there were angles on her face where there hadn't been angles before.

'Let me in, Cat,' he said grimly. 'Please.'

Catrin flinched, knowing she ought to refuse, but she opened the door anyway. It was pointless to engage in a battle you stood no chance of winning and she was too weary to try. He had come all this way—had stepped outside his usual luxurious habitat to find himself in the staff quarters of a Welsh seaside hotel. She could hardly turn him away.

'Okay,' she said. 'But please keep the noise down. Some of my colleagues are on night duty and some might still be asleep. I don't want you making some kind of racket and waking them up.'

Murat's mouth hardened as he stepped inside the room. It was clean but it was also very cramped, and he thought how bare it looked. Why, even the servants at his palace in Qurhah had better accommodation than this. On a small dressing table, he could see that over-sized hairbrush she always used to rake through her thick hair, along with a framed photograph of her and her sister. As always, there was an open book on a locker beside the narrow bed and, on the wall, an ugly notice warning inhabitants what to do in case of fire.

Finishing his brief reconnoitre, he returned his

gaze to her face but he could do absolutely nothing about the sudden protective clenching of his heart. She looked as if a light breeze might be enough to make her float away.

He walked over to the small window and looked out onto a yard filled with bins, before turning back—his black eyes narrowed in question. 'Why did you run out on me in Italy like that?'

'You know the answer to that question—so please don't insult my intelligence by pretending you don't. I went because I needed to get away and I didn't want to have to ask your permission. I'm a free agent now and I look after myself.'

'You didn't think I'd be worried?'

'Funnily enough, your reaction wasn't the biggest thing on my mind. For once, it wasn't about you, Murat. It was about me.' The effort of saying so much had tired her out and she sat down on the bed and leaned back against the pillows. 'What are you doing here?'

Once again, he swept his gaze over the small room, countering her question with one of his own. 'Why have you come back to Wales?'

'Because of...family reasons.' Rather defensively, she stared at him. 'I like it. It's a decent enough hotel and quite adequate for my needs. How did you find me?'

'A person can always be found.'

'That doesn't answer my question.'

'The answer isn't important. I have means at my disposal—you know that. What matters is why you're here.' His black eyes narrowed. 'What kind of family reasons?'

She shook her head. 'It doesn't matter.'

'Yes, it does.'

She had forgotten about his stubborn nature and autocratic determination to get his own way. She'd forgotten that, a few minutes in his company, she would be longing for him to hold her in his arms again. She pushed a strand of hair away from her hot cheek and met the question which was lancing from his eyes.

And why was she resisting telling him? Wouldn't the truth kill off any residual dreams of romance for good—and send him running from here at the speed of light? Was that what she was secretly afraid of?

Catrin felt a sudden rush of nerves constricting her throat as the inevitable moment of revelation approached. If only she were somebody different, it might not have mattered. If she'd been one of those high-born aristocratic women with bishops and artists in her lineage, then an eccentric relative would have been perfectly acceptable.

But she wasn't.

She was just ordinary Catrin Thomas, who always dreaded this moment more than any other. She hated the shame and the pity which always hardened people's eyes when they found out. And she would have given anything not to see it in Murat's.

'My sister asked me to come back to Wales to help with my mother, who is…sick.'

A frowning look of consternation crossed over his face. 'Then why on earth didn't you just say so?'

She didn't answer for a moment.

'Cat?'

'Because it's not the kind of illness you want to shout from the rooftops,' she said. 'My mother is…'

'Your mother is what?' Murat prompted and now his voice sounded almost gentle and, in an awful way, that made it worse. She didn't want him being gentle, or understanding or any of those things he wasn't supposed to be. She wanted him to be hard and stern and autocratic, because surely that would help prepare her for the revulsion which he'd be unable to disguise when eventually she told him.

'She's an alcoholic.'

Her bald words sounded brittle and sour, and it took a moment or two before she could bear to look into his eyes. And when she did they were hard. Hard as unpolished chips of jet. Just as she'd known they would be all along.

'Explain,' he said curtly.

Her clenched fingers wouldn't seem to stop shaking. 'It doesn't require much in the way of explanation. My mother is a drunk. She…she drinks in a way that other people don't. She doesn't know when to stop, or, rather, she *can't* stop. She's one of those people for whom one sip is too many, and a million not enough. She can't…' She shrugged, trying to do the acceptance thing again. But sometimes acceptance was difficult when it made you face what was breaking your heart. She drew in a deep breath and it was only with an effort borne out of years of practice which stopped her voice from breaking down completely. 'She can't help herself. She loves to drink, but one day it will k-kill her. She's been on yet another binge. It started weeks ago—that's why I came back from Italy so suddenly. And living closer means that I can help out when there's another catastrophe—which seems to be most of the time.'

He didn't speak at first and when he did his words were so quiet that she had to strain her ears to hear them.

'I see.'

'You're shocked,' she said numbly.

'Of course I'm shocked—but mainly because it's such a startling thing to discover at this stage of knowing you. I'm wondering why you never told me any of this before,' he said. His black gaze bored into her. 'Why not, Cat?'

Wearily, she lifted her palm to her hot brow in a failed attempt to cool it down. 'Because we didn't have that kind of relationship, did we? Our pillow talk never really got personal. Your life in Qurhah was completely separate and mine in Wales was the same. You never asked me questions about my past and I guess I liked it that way.'

But she knew that wasn't the whole truth and something inside tugged at her conscience. Made her want him to see things as *she* had seen them. 'Plus we mustn't forget that you're a sultan,' she continued hoarsely. 'And I was afraid.'

Her words tailed off and he looked at her.

'What were you afraid of?'

Once she wouldn't have dreamed of telling him
this. When she was trying to be that perfect woman
who never wanted to bring any stress into his life.
When she was trying to be what she thought he
wanted her to be. But now she was free. She might
be relatively poor and worried sick about the future,
but at least she was free to speak her mind.

'I was afraid you would dump me if you found
out.'

He gave a short laugh. 'You really think I'm that
shallow?'

'I think maybe sultans are forced to be shallow.'
She gave another hacking cough. 'Otherwise why
choose a bride just because she happened to be a
royal virgin? A sultan certainly couldn't ever marry
a woman whose mother might turn up drunk, w-with
bottles of liquor clinking in a brown paper bag.'

Murat didn't answer. Not at first. He was too busy
absorbing the significance of what she had told him.
But currently her words were of far less concern
than the wild light which was filling her eyes with
a strange green fire—so that her skin looked as if it
was bathed in an unearthly glow.

Walking over to the bed, he leaned over to put the
back of his hand on her forehead, frowning as her
teeth began to chatter. 'What have you been doing
to yourself, Cat? You're sick.'

She coughed again and this time her whole frame
was wracked with paroxysms. 'It's just a cold.'

'It is not just a cold. It's a damned fever.'

'Whatever.' Cat could feel the light touch of his hand on her clammy brow as new waves of dizziness swept over her. Suddenly, the chattering was making her teeth hurt and she felt as if ice had started creeping around her veins. She started trying to pull the duvet out from beneath her but her fingers were fumbling too much. 'I'm c-cold.'

'You are not cold,' he said grimly. 'You are burning up.'

'I want the duvet.'

'Not now, Cat,' he said. 'Stop fighting. Let me deal with this.'

His soft command lulled her as it had lulled her so often in the past. Her head fell back against the lumpy pillow and her weighted eyelids began to close, until she felt his fingers at the fly of her jeans and her eyes flew open.

'What do you think you're doing?'

'You think I'm so desperate that I'd take advantage of a sick woman?' His voice was bitter; his mouth a contemptuous slash. 'Let me assure you that I have nothing but your welfare in mind right now—and it's clear that, while you may have been helping care for your mother, you certainly haven't been looking after yourself.'

She wanted to tell him not to bother, but she couldn't. All she could do was lie there like a piece of meat on a block as he began to undress her, like some awful parody of the way he had undressed her countless times before. But there was no softness or appreciation in his touch now. She was aware of him tugging at her zip and slithering the jeans down over her hot thighs in a way which was almost clinical.

And suddenly, she was too woozy to care. Even when he peeled off her T-shirt and one of her breasts brushed against his palm as if it had been programmed to do so. Through the haze of her growing fever, she sensed his momentary hesitation. As if he was remembering how once he would have dragged his thumb across her bra to incite the puckering nub.

But he withdrew his hand as if he had accidentally plunged it into a pit of snakes. And it hurt to think that now he was repulsed by her, when once he hadn't been able to get enough of her.

Feeling like an unwanted sacrifice, Catrin lay there in her bra and pants, while Murat withdrew his phone from his pocket and began to speak in rapid Qurhahian.

# CHAPTER TEN

CAT SWAM IN and out of a strange and swamping fever which seemed to have taken her prisoner. She remembered feeling cold. Freezing cold. But she was forced to curl up into a foetal position, because Murat was stubbornly refusing to let her cover herself with the duvet.

Murat?

Was she delirious?

No. It seemed she was not. Her eyes flickered open to see the hawk-like Sultan sitting beside her bed, his dark body very still and watchful. Murat was in her room. He was filling the tiny space as if it were his *right* to be there.

'Why are you still here?' she heard herself mumble at some point. 'Didn't I tell you to go?'

'You did. Repeatedly. But I'm here and this is where I'm staying. Looking after you, if you must know—since you seem incapable of taking care of yourself.'

'I don't need you,' she muttered.

'It's not up for discussion, and I'm not going any-where until you're better. Better get used to it, Cat.'

He was so bossy, she thought crossly. He was making her drink water when she didn't want to drink anything—glasses and glasses of the stuff. And he was wringing out that little flannel she kept draped over the small sink. Wringing it out in cold water and making her yelp as he rubbed the icy cloth over her protesting skin.

Some time, through the awful pounding which had resumed inside her head, she heard someone knocking at the door and then a low conversation taking place in a language she recognised instantly as Qurhahian. And that was when Murat walked over to the bed, holding a small and golden phial, which he lifted to her lips.

'Drink this,' he commanded.

Through bleary eyes, she gazed at him suspiciously. 'Is it some sort of poison?'

'You think I'd feed you poison?'

'Nothing about you would surprise me.'

'Drink it, Cat,' he said gently. 'It'll make you feel better.'

But it didn't. It made her feel worse. Thick and viscous, it clung to her throat and was so bitter that she would have spat it out if Murat hadn't held her lips together and forced her to swallow.

'Don't do that,' she said from between gritted teeth.

'Then drink it.'

'It tastes disgusting! Like carpet slippers!'

'Not a taste I am familiar with. So why not close your eyes and pretend it's something else? What would you like it to taste like, *habibti*?'

He was luring her into the realm of fantasy as he'd done so often in the past, and Catrin screwed her eyes against the light and the pain and the awful ache in her heart. He used to call her *habibti* when he was making love to her. *Habibti* when he was stroking her hair…

'I'd like it to taste like warm, buttered toast,' she said, thinking of a book she used to read as a child beneath the bedclothes, while her mother was crashing around downstairs. She remembered how comforting it had been to escape into the land of fantasy. How the books had allowed her to forget the harsh reality of her real life. Her voice grew dreamy. 'Or hot chocolate with marshmallows and cream, and chocolate sprinkles on the top.'

'What else?' he prompted, his voice very gentle again.

'Turkish delight by the Christmas tree,' she continued. 'And snow falling outside and making everything silent.'

By the time she'd finished speaking, all the liquid was swallowed and her eyelids were growing heavy. Through the flickering curtain of her quivering eyelashes, she could see the watchful gleam of his black eyes.

'I'm tired now,' she said.

'Then sleep.'

She did. One minute she was drenched in sweat

and the next she felt as if she were floating outside
her body, looking down on the tiny room. While all
the time, Murat sat beside her bed, like some gran-
ite-faced sentry. The only time he moved was when
she needed to use the bathroom and he shrugged
her into the robe which was hanging on the back of
the door and carried her along the corridor. But she
was too woozy to care about the unexpected intimacy of even *that*.

Afterwards he took her back to her room and
laid her on the bed and she looked up at him as he
smoothed back her matted hair. She could feel that
stupid great flare of love welling up inside her and
wondered why it hadn't left her, as she had been
praying so hard for it to do. But he had been kind
to her, hadn't he? More than kind. And kindness
could be seductive too—the most seductive thing
in the world.

'Thank you,' she said, and fell into a deep sleep.

When she awoke it must have been morning, because a chill grey light was coming in through the
windows and Murat hadn't moved from the chair
he'd been sitting in. He didn't even appear to have
slept, for his gaze was sharp and alert as soon as
she opened her eyes. Only the new beard at his jaw
and the dark shadows hollowing his cheeks gave any
indication that he must have been there for hours.

*And she was lying there in her bra and pants!*

Surreptitiously, she reached down for the duvet
and hauled it over herself and saw him give a flicker
of a smile.

'This is the bit where you say "what happened?",' he said, handing her a glass of water.

'What happened?' she questioned, propping herself up on her elbows to gulp it down, achingly aware of him and his proximity.

'You were sick and now you're better.'

Fragments of the night came filtering back. The way he'd pushed away those strands of sweaty hair from her brow. The way he'd carried her. She tried to push the image away. To think about things which wouldn't make her realise how much she'd missed him. 'I do remember. You gave me something disgusting to drink.'

'I agree that taste-wise it's not up there with nectar,' he said wryly. 'That was what we call a *Dimdar*. It's an old desert remedy made from the sap of a rare cactus which grows in the Mekathasinian Sands, and which desert warriors have been using for centuries to treat their ailments.'

She was horribly aware that the inside of her mouth felt gritty and stale. 'I need a shower.'

'I'm not stopping you.'

But she felt horribly vulnerable as she struggled out of bed. As if she'd been caught with all her defences down and she wasn't sure how best to erect them again. Grabbing an armful of clothes, she went along the corridor to the communal bathroom, but the face which stared back at her from the mirror confirmed her worst fears. She touched the sweat-soaked tendrils of her hair, which hung around her pinched face. Murat had seen her like this. Unwashed and pale and looking nothing like the woman he had once lived with.

She told herself she was no longer his arm-candy, nor was she trying to impress him. Nonetheless, she spent a long time in the sputtering shower, half expecting him to be gone by the time she returned to her room. He hadn't, of course, and she blinked at the scene which greeted her. He had made the bed and boiled the kettle and was now pouring boiling water into two mugs, in which bobbed a couple of teabags. It made such a comforting yet incongruous image, that for a moment she felt as if she were right back in the middle of her delirium.

He glanced up as she walked in, his black eyes lingering on her for a moment longer than was necessary. 'You look better,' he commented.

'That wouldn't be difficult. I feel much better.' She put her damp towel in the linen basket, knowing what she needed to say. But it felt strange to be doing so without her arms looped around his neck or her lips brushing against that unshaven jaw. 'I want to thank you for what you did.'

'It was nothing.'

'Yes, it was.' She tried to concentrate on the situation as it *was*, rather than what she wanted it to be. She suddenly realised why he'd once told her that he wasn't in the habit of seducing virgins. *Their dreams are still intact.* And hers had been, hadn't they? No matter how hard she'd tried to convince herself that she didn't do the dream stuff—she could see now that she had been deluding herself. She'd believed that she was immune to emotion because she had wanted to believe it and because it had allowed her to buy a ticket into his life. He'd wanted a no-strings affair and she'd convinced herself that she was happy to go along with that. But maybe at heart she was just a woman who'd been longing for him to commit to her all along.

'I'm very grateful for all you've done, but I won't take up any more of your time,' she said, watching him squeeze out a teabag. 'There must be something important needing your attention.'

'I can take care of my own timetable, Cat,' he said, handing her a mug of tea. 'I want you to tell me about your mother.'

She felt her cheeks growing red. 'I told you everything last night.'

He shook his head. 'Not really. You spoke in terms of a problem, but not in terms of a solution. Has she ever tried rehab?'

'Rehab's expensive.'

'So that's a no?'

'Of course it's a no!' she bit back. 'We're ordinary people, Murat. Where do you suppose we could find that kind of money?'

His eyes didn't leave her face. 'You could have asked me.'

'But that would have involved telling you—and I didn't want to tell you, for reasons you can probably understand.'

'I'd like to meet her,' he said suddenly.

'Well, you can't.'

'What are you so scared of, Cat?'

Surely even *he* knew the answer to that. She didn't want to see the disgust on his face when he saw just how sordid her home life had been. And it wasn't fair of him to want to intrude on her life like this. Because this wasn't what happened in their particular relationship. They had separate lives. Separate futures.

Yet as she saw a familiar look of determination glinting from his eyes, she wondered what she was trying to protect herself from. She didn't have to try to impress him any more. It was *over*. It didn't matter how many of her dark secrets he discovered, did it?

'If you want to meet my mother then we'll go and meet her,' she said. 'When did you have in mind?'

'How about now?' His gaze searched her face. 'That is, if you're feeling well enough.'

Her throat constricted. 'She won't be expecting us. She won't have had time to tidy the place up.' She said the words as if she came from a normal house. As if she had the kind of mother who had ever bothered tidying up.

'I don't care,' said Murat. 'And before you say anything, I'd actually enjoy making an impromptu visit for once. Do you have any idea what usually happens when I plan a trip somewhere? How entire rooms are repainted and new furniture bought?'

'You're unlikely to get anything like that at my mother's house,' she said flippantly. 'You'll be lucky to get fresh milk, let alone fresh paint.'

His expression didn't change. 'Shall we go?'

'Well, you've asked for it,' she said as she looked round the room for her shoes.

She locked the door behind them and followed him down to the hotel car park, where his two black limousines were inciting a lot of interest.

In no time at all they had left the little seaside town and were driving past fields blurred with rain and dotted with the dripping forms of motionless sheep. She saw the grey buildings of villages and sometimes the fluttering of the distinctive Welsh flag, with its proud scarlet dragon set on a green and white background. The car picked up speed as they headed south, until tall columns of factory chimneys began to appear in the distance.

At last their small convoy entered a street which was barely wide enough to accommodate the width of the two cars. Rows of tiny identical houses lay before them and Catrin tried to imagine what they must look like to Murat's eyes. Did he see the stray piece of garbage which drifted over the pavement, or notice the peeling paintwork on her mother's front door?

She dreaded what the inside of the house would look like. If her sister was still here, then at least she could have relied on the place looking halfway respectable. But Rachel was now back at Uni and, while grateful that she was out of the inevitable firing line, Catrin was a mass of nerves as she rang the doorbell.

At first there was a pause so long that she wondered if her mother was down at the local pub. And didn't part of her pray that was the case? So that they could just go away and this awful meeting would never happen? But she could hear the distant sound of the TV, and the slow shuffle of footsteps which greeted Murat's second ring told her that her hopes were in vain.

The door opened and Ursula Thomas stood there, swaying a little as she peered at them—her stained and scruffy clothes failing to hide a faint paunch. Her once beautiful features were coarsened and ruddy, and the emerald eyes so like her daughter's were heavily bloodshot. And just as she did pretty much every time she saw her, Catrin felt the inevitable wave of sadness which washed over her as she looked at her mother. What a waste, she thought. *What a waste of a life.*

'Catrin?' Ursula said, her gaze focusing and then refocusing.

'Yes, Mum. It's me. And I've brought a…friend to see you. Murat, this is Ursula—my mother. Mum, this is Murat.'

Ursula looked up at Murat and gave him a vacant smile. 'You haven't got a smoke on you by any chance?' she said.

Catrin half expected Murat to turn around and walk straight back to his car, but he did no such thing. Instead, he shrugged his broad shoulders as if people asked him such things every day of the week.

'Not on me, I'm afraid,' he said. 'May we come in?'

Ursula looked him up and down before opening the door to let them in.

As they picked their way over the discarded
shoes and empty plastic bags which were littering
the small hallway Catrin watched as Murat followed
her mother into a tiny sitting room which reeked of
stale smoke. On a small table next to a faded armchair stood a half-empty tumbler of vodka. Beside
the glass was a crumpled cigarette packet and an
overflowing ashtray. A game show blared out from
the giant TV screen and the sound of the canned
studio laughter added a surreal touch to the bizarre
meeting.

Catrin wanted to curl up and die but her shame
lasted only as long as it took for her self-worth to
assert itself. Because *she* had done nothing to be
ashamed of. This was not her house, nor her mess.
And Ursula was ill, not wicked.

She glanced up at Murat but the expression on his
hawkish face gave nothing away. He glanced down
to meet her eyes and gave her the faintest of smiles.

'I wonder if you'd mind going out to buy a packet
of cigarettes, Cat?' he questioned calmly. 'While I
have a talk to your mother.'

The request threw her. Confused her. She wanted
to refuse, but something told her that refusal wasn't
an option.

'Okay,' she said, and left her mother blinking in
some bewilderment as she realised she was going to
be left alone with the towering figure of the Sultan.

Catrin let herself out onto the narrow street and
sucked in some of the damp, cool air. On the other
side of the street, she saw a curtain twitch and she

turned to trace some of the old, familiar steps of her childhood. The little corner shop was still there, hanging on despite the inexorable march of the out-of-town hypermarket, and she bought a pack of cigarettes and a carton of milk.

She didn't have a clue what Murat was going to say to her mother but right then she didn't care, because she trusted him to do the right thing. He might have been emotionally closed down as a partner, but she'd read enough about Qurhah to know that he was revered as a ruler, both at home and abroad. And in truth, wasn't it a comfort to have someone else taking over like this, even if it was only for a short while? Hadn't the burden of responsibility always fallen on *her*?

She'd spent her life trying to shield Rachel from the fall-out of this sordid and erratic life. She'd cooked meals from store-cupboard scraps and bought food at the end of the day from the nearby market, when they were practically giving the stuff away. She'd known survival in bucket-loads, but she'd never known *comfort*. She had always been prepared for the final demands landing on the doormat. Or the telephone being cut off because the money put aside for the bill had been drunk away.

Maybe that was what had made her so determined to hang onto what Murat had offered her. Like some urchin who'd spent her life shivering outside in the cold, hadn't she also been attracted by his lifestyle, which had cushioned her in unfamiliar luxury?

By the time she got back with the cigarettes, she

found her mother slumped in the armchair, but the ashtray had been emptied and the glass of vodka replaced by a mug of black coffee. Murat emerged from the kitchen, his jacket removed and his shirt-sleeves rolled up.

'What's going on?' Catrin questioned, handing her mother the packet of cigarettes and watching as she began to tear at the cellophane wrapping with trembling fingers.

'Your mother has agreed to go into rehab,' he said.

Waiting for the stream of objection which didn't come, Catrin narrowed her eyes. 'How can she?'

'I wonder if I could have a word with you, Cat?' Murat's voice cut through her words as easily as a hot knife slicing through butter. 'In private.'

She joined him in the kitchen where, to her astonishment, he had started making inroads into the enormous pile of filthy dishes which were piled up in the sink. Shutting the door behind her, she stared at him in confusion.

'Is this for real?'

He nodded. 'Completely.'

She swallowed, not wanting to believe it. 'What did you say to her to get her to agree to something like that?'

'I repeated exactly what you told me. I said that she was going to kill herself if she carried on that way.' His black gaze was very steady. 'I think I managed to convince her that you and your sister would be completely devastated were that to happen. I told her that you'd both already suffered enough by watching her wreck her life and her health. I asked if she wanted to save herself, before it was too late. And then I said that I was prepared to pay for her to go into a rehabilitation unit.'

Wildly, Catrin shook her head. 'I can't let you do that,' she said. 'I looked into it once. It costs thousands of pounds.'

'Which I can easily afford, as we both know. The money isn't important.' He stepped forward, stemming her objection by placing a forefinger over her lips. 'Let me do it, Cat. I want to.'

Angrily, she jerked her mouth away from the touch of that distracting finger, hating the fact that her body could react to him even in moments like this. '*Why?* You don't even *know* my mother.'

'I think we both know why. For you.'

'As a kind of pay-off?' she questioned bitterly.

'That's one way of looking at it, I suppose, although I'd prefer not to think of what we shared in terms of money.'

'Really? Don't you think you're being rather naïve? It was a *transaction*, Murat,' she said. 'You know it was.'

He flinched, but the gaze he fixed on her face was steady. 'Let's not quibble about what our relationship was, or wasn't. Let's just think about your mother. Surely she deserves this chance?' he persisted. 'Especially when I can send her to the best place money can buy.'

Catrin pursed her lips together. Of course he could. Murat could buy anything he pleased. Anything and anyone. *He had bought her, hadn't he?* Purchased her just as surely as if he'd walked into a store and asked for a woman who would be willing to begin a brand-new life as his mistress. And she had gone along with it. She'd almost bitten his hand off in her eagerness.

But just because her easy acceptance of that role now appalled her—was it really fair to refuse her mother this one last chance?

She thought of the woman sitting slumped in the armchair next door, her whole world centred around a bottle of liquor and her health declining year on year. She thought about the way her own heart froze every time the phone rang, wondering if this was going to be the call she'd spent her whole life dreading. Was she going to allow her own wounded pride to stop her from accepting this potential lifeline which might just save her mother?

She looked into Murat's face, as stern and as implacable now as she'd ever seen it. Her gaze travelled down to the whorls of hairs on his powerful forearms, all damp from where he'd been washing up. He was *trying*, she realised. He was doing the best he could. He might not be able to offer *her* anything in the way of a future but he was using his considerable power to reach out and help her mother. What right did she have to turn that help down, just because her heart was broken?

'Yes, of course she deserves it,' she said stiffly. 'And if you really mean it then I'd like to accept your kind offer.'

'Good.' He nodded. 'Then let's put that in motion straight away.'

She hesitated. 'I know I must have sounded like an ungrateful, spoilt brat just now, but I wasn't really thinking straight.'

'Spoilt?' At this he gave a flat laugh. 'I've known plenty of spoiled women in my life, Cat, but that is one description I wouldn't dream of applying to you. If you're agreeable, I can make a few phone calls while you help your mother to pack and then I'll take you back to the hotel.'

## CHAPTER ELEVEN

'BEFORE I SAY goodbye, I want…' Catrin cleared her throat and tried again. 'I want to say something. You've been so kind to my mother, Murat. More than kind. And I don't know how I can ever possibly thank you.'

In the faintly tinted light of the limousine, Murat looked into Cat's screwed-up face—guessing how much those unsteady words had cost her to say.

He thought back to the scene which had greeted him at her mother's house. He had seen much during desert warfare which had shocked him, but he had been completely taken aback by the squalor he'd encountered there. He wondered if subconsciously Cat had rebelled against that childhood squalor and whether that had been one of the reasons why she'd become such an exemplary homemaker.

He prayed that his intervention with her mother would work, because he knew that addicts had a notoriously poor rate of recovery. He had sensed Cat's anxiety as they had waited for the doctor's car which was to take Ursula Thomas to the airport and ulti-

mately to the rehab unit in Arizona. And he had
sensed her hope, too. He had seen her struggling to
hold onto her composure as she had gently helped her
mother into the back of the car. He tried to imagine
the child she must have been, growing up with that
constant sense of chaos and terror. Having to protect her younger sister from all the confusion which
surrounded them. His heart had clenched then, with
pain for all she must have experienced, and frustration that nobody had been there to help her.

She had spent most of the journey back to the
hotel in silence, looking out of the window as if she'd
never seen those rain-soft views before. But now that
they were here, she had no choice but to look at him
and he could sense her reluctance to do so. Was it his
imagination, or were those cactus-green eyes suspiciously bright? Was she close to tears? He wouldn't
know. Over the years he had been subjected to the
tearful displays of many women, often provoked by
his refusal to do what they wanted. But this particular woman had never once cried in front of him.

Yet she, more than most, had cause to.

She had kept so much hidden from him…though
at last he could understand why. Hers was not the
kind of background you'd want to shout about from
the rooftops—especially to a man who came from
one of the oldest and proudest dynasties in the world.
And he had never pressed her, had he? Arrogantly, he
had breathed a sigh of relief that she hadn't been one
of those women who wanted to yank out every emotion and memory, and then analyse them to death.

He kept his eyes fixed on her pale face. 'I don't know that I'm ready to say goodbye just yet. Are you?'

Catrin blinked rapidly until she was certain that she wasn't going to let herself down by bursting into tears, though she wasn't sure how much longer she could keep it together. If she got out of the car now, she could make it safely back to her room and nobody but her would see her cry.

Yet didn't part of her want to extend this bit for as long as possible? Because she knew that this really would be the last time she would ever see Murat. He would never come into her life again after today.

Her heart gave a little twist of pain. He had returned because he had been worried about her and had discovered much more than he'd ever bargained for. The stark differences between them had been revealed with much greater clarity than she would have chosen. But now he could turn his back on her for good, his conscience clear. He had done his duty. He had helped her mother—and now the slate was wiped perfectly clean.

This was the last time she would ever stare into that face—a hard face which disguised his surprising kindness and even—she bit her lip—a *gentleness* which had made her heart want to melt. He had not judged her mother but had simply sought a practical solution to her dilemma, and for that she would be grateful to him for ever.

Yet she wasn't quite ready to say goodbye either.

Like him, she wanted to prolong it, just a bit more. 'We could go and have coffee if you like,' she said.

His dark brows knitted together. 'In your room?'

'No, not there,' she said quickly. It was too small. Too *intimate*. And there was a bed there, wasn't there? She didn't want to be anywhere near a bed. She didn't trust herself not to make a fool of herself one last time. What if she found herself begging him to hold her close, so that she could feel his hard body warm against hers? Maybe she might even be weak enough to have sex with him one last time. 'There's a little place, near here. Down by the harbour. We could go there.'

He nodded and pressed a button so that the interconnecting glass slid open and Catrin leaned forward and gave directions to the driver.

The light changed as they approached the quayside and she could see the bobbing of the boats in the distance. It was another reason why she had come back to work in this area. Putting her mother's illness aside, living here was no hardship. A cheap little Welsh seaside town she'd once visited on a school trip and which she had never forgotten.

She remembered that it had been a day when, for once, she'd felt just like any other child. She had eaten ice cream and paddled in the sea and the water had been so cold that her legs had turned blue. But she recalled her exhilaration and the sense of freedom, and she'd held onto that memory for a long, long time. The people who still came here on holiday didn't have lots of money to spend, but Catrin still liked it here. The sea was the sea wherever you went, and she thought the small harbour was as pretty as any Murat had taken her to in Europe. It was certainly a much cheaper place to buy a cup of coffee.

'Let's leave the car up here, out of sight,' she said as they got out into the drizzle and she pointed down the steep road towards the glitter of the waves.

'Why?' questioned Murat.

She shrugged. 'Because this is a small town and I don't want people wondering what I was doing in a car like this. They might draw their own conclusions—some of them not very nice—and I'd rather they didn't.'

Murat reflected that this was the first time in his life when his credentials *hadn't* been paraded in an attempt to obtain some reflected royal glory. He turned to look at her, noting that her skin was pale and her eyes smudged by shadows, and suddenly it felt as if an iron fist had been clamped around his heart. He wanted to cradle her and to hold her close. He wanted to kiss her hair and her eyes and her lips. But he knew that he couldn't keep taking from her and giving nothing back.

'But you've been ill,' he said harshly. 'I don't think you should be walking anywhere.'

'I'm fine. Your *Dimdar* worked like magic, and, besides, what would the alternative be? Are you proposing to carry me down there?'

'If you like. I'd carry you in an instant, Cat,' he said. 'You only have to say the word.'

'Don't be ridiculous,' she said, but she knew he

meant it. Murat came from the kind of world where men were definitely men, and would scoop up a woman into their arms if the need arose. She re-alised that he was as much a protector as a king. And all these things made her love him more.

*And I don't want to love him. It hurts too much to keep loving him.*

It was one of those cold September days which gave a chill foreshadowing of the winter to come. A thin wind whipped the leaves from the trees and her ponytailed hair flew behind her. As they approached the small harbour she could see the cascade of frothy white waves and hear the mournful cries of seagulls as they circled overhead.

The café was very basic. The mugs were thick and the tea too strong. What usually sold the place to Catrin was the view, but today it was difficult to get enthusiastic about the water outside, or the clouds billowing like smoke in a gunmetal sky.

She slid into a chair opposite Murat and wondered if he'd ever sat at a scratched Formica table before, with bottles of tomato sauce and vinegar in front of him. She watched as he tipped two small sachets of sugar into his tea, the white granules flowing like the sands of time, and she was reminded of that first time she'd ever met him when he had dipped a sugar cube into his coffee and sucked it.

Why remember that now? she asked herself fiercely. How is it going to help if you reinforce how attractive you found him? Wrong tense. Find him. Wrong tense again. Will always find him.

Aware of the mother and toddler at a nearby table, she spoke in a low voice. 'I want to thank—'

'No,' he interrupted, his voice just as low. 'Please don't. You've thanked me enough and we've said everything I want to say on that particular subject. Now, all we can do is pray that the treatment works. We have very little time left, Cat, and I don't want to waste a second of it. Not when I suspect that you have spent more years than anyone should, worrying about your mother.'

His remarks were thoughtful and perceptive, but they didn't really help. It wasn't going to aid her own recovery if she carried on thinking of him as her knight in shining armour. So think of the reality. Think what he's been doing since last time you saw him.

'So how have you been?' she said. 'During your time back in Qurhah?'

He gave a faint smile. 'Mostly good. There is relative peace in the region at the moment and our exports are up. I'm heralding a drive to build new schools in the east of the kingdom.'

'That's all very commendable, Murat,' she said quietly. 'But that wasn't what I meant.'

'No.' There was a pause. 'I guess it wasn't.'

'How *is* the hunt for a suitable bride going?' she questioned brightly. 'Has any particular candidate caught your eye?'

'Cat, don't.'

'Don't what?' She tilted her head to one side and

looked at him quizzically. 'Don't face facts? Don't square up to the truth of what's really happening?'

'I don't want to discuss it. Especially not with you.'

'But I do,' she persisted. 'I really do. Think of it as an exercise in letting go. It helps me realise what your real life is like, rather than allowing myself to construct fantasies about what it might have been like. Have you...' She stirred her tea, even though it contained no sugar. 'Have you seen many women?'

He leaned back in his chair. 'Not many. Some.'

'And those you have seen, what of them? Were their feet too big for the glass slipper, or was there some other reason why they wouldn't make a suitable royal bride?'

He gave the briefest of smiles before a hard look entered his eyes and then he thought, Damn you, Cat. Did she think he was finding this easy? *Did she?* 'One of the problems is that I require a virgin, but unfortunately many of these princesses are not. Some of them have been away to school in Europe and America, and have entered into relationships with other men.'

Catrin put her mug down on the table with a clatter. 'I can't believe you just said that. All these years you've steadily been working your way through scores of beautiful women. You've probably got more notches on your bedpost than the average Hollywood stud, yet you expect your future bride to behave as if we're still living in the Middle Ages. Do you have any idea how much of a hypocrite you sound?'

'I am not judging these women for the sake of judging them,' he bit out. 'But it is my *duty* to marry a virgin princess! That is what is decreed in the Qurhahian statute, as it has always been decreed.'

'But times change, and so do people. In every way. Think about it, Murat.' Pushing the mug out of the way, she leaned forward, her elbows resting on the Formica table. 'Once, your country relied solely on oil for energy, you exported it and you used it, you told me that yourself. But now you've expanded into wind farms and you said that you're investing in solar energy as well.'

'This much is true,' he conceded.

'Years ago, you would have relied on messengers riding on horseback across the desert to relay news but now you use the Internet and telephones, just like everyone else. I remember you telling me about that guy you brought in to shake up Qurhah's international profile—the one who ended up marrying your sister.'

'Gabe Steel,' he said automatically.

'That's right. And you told me what a brilliant job he did. But hasn't it occurred to you that you've modernised everything except the man at the top—you? You've moved with the times and yet you're sticking to some outdated law which says that you've got to marry a virgin, when hardly anyone is these days.'

'But you were,' he said suddenly. 'You were.'

His words swiftly brought her to her senses and Catrin's mouth closed, her objections fizzling away to nothing as she wondered what on earth she was trying to do here. Was she trying to argue her corner in some mistaken belief that Murat would consider taking *her* as a bride? Did she really think that was ever going to happen—especially now, when he'd just seen what dodgy genes she had?

'I'm sorry,' she said. 'It's none of my business. You must marry who you choose.'

He leaned forward himself, mirroring her own elbowed pose, so that their faces were close as they looked at one another across the table.

'But if I could choose with my heart rather than with my head, then I would choose you, Cat,' he said softly. 'Because you are the woman I love.'

Her heart gave a hard and painful beat. 'Don't.'

'I must. I need you to understand,' he said. 'No matter what happens, I need you to know what you mean to me.'

'Murat…'

'Because after everything that has happened, I owe you this much,' he said, then took a deep breath. 'You captivated me from the first moment I set eyes on you. You fulfilled every fantasy I'd ever had. You were beautiful and spirited and, yes, you were a virgin, too—and I will not lie when I tell you how much that meant to me, once I'd got over my initial shock. So I brought you back to London with me, not thinking beyond the first month or even the first week.'

'Neither was I,' she whispered.

He lifted his fingertips to her face, running them down over her cheek and Catrin could do nothing to stop herself from shivering beneath his touch.

'I had never lived with a woman before you,' he said. 'And I suppose if I'm being really honest maybe I was trying it out for size. Seeing what it was like to share your life with someone.'

Like test-driving a new car, thought Catrin, but she didn't say anything.

'And then you changed,' he said. 'Maybe that was inevitable. I don't know. You became more...polished. It was like a transformation. You fitted into my life so well. More than you should have done. Living with you was easy, maybe too easy, and I guess we were just drifting along.'

'And then I found out about your secret courtship.'

'Yes,' he said. 'And you were furious—rightly so. And that was when you stopped being the textbook mistress. You stopped being the smooth, unflappable Cat I had become used to. You became the Cat I had fallen for all that time ago. Fiery Cat. Outspoken Cat. You showed me your claws, Cat. You scratched me and drew blood, and I...I found myself falling in love with you.'

Catrin pulled away, sitting back and locking her trembling fingers together, because this was terrible. Terrible and wonderful all at the same time, because it was all too late. 'Why on earth are you telling me all this?' she whispered. 'And why *now*?'

'Because I want you to know how I feel about you,' he said. 'I need you to know that I love you. Very much. I love you in a way I hadn't thought myself capable of. But I am. And I do.'

She received the words in disbelieving silence,

wondering if she dared tell him that she felt exactly the same way. Or had he guessed a long time ago that a woman would never behave as she had behaved unless she also loved?

But she was cautious. He had hurt her before and he was capable of still hurting her. 'What is it you're saying?' she questioned boldly. 'That we have some kind of future together?'

He shook his head and swallowed. 'Not the kind of future which another man will one day be able to offer you,' he said, and now his face looked as if it had been carved from some cold, dark stone. 'I can't marry you, Cat, no matter how much I might wish that I could. And anyway, it is all academic now. Because my advisors in Qurhah have informed me…' there was a pause while he seemed to be struggling to find the right words '…have informed me that a perfect bride has at last been found. Apparently, she fulfils all the criteria.'

Catrin was grateful that she hadn't eaten, because for one brief moment she honestly thought she might throw up. And that thought was quickly followed by the desire to punch him. How dared he raise her hopes like that and then smash them down again? She wanted to beat her fists hard against his chest and demand to know whether he took some kind of perverse pleasure from engaging in a sadistic form of torture…

But she quashed that instinct and relied instead on the cool logic she had become so good at. He was being honest, that was all. She couldn't complain when he didn't tell her what was going on his life and then moan when he *did*, just because she didn't like it.

He had cared for her when she'd been sick. He had provided her mother with a bail-out package and sent her to an expensive clinic in Arizona. He had let down his guard enough to tell her that he loved her and she knew him well enough to recognise that such an admission would not have come easily. He was a good man, not a bad man. A man who was governed by a strong sense of duty and doing the right thing for the country he served.

She couldn't blame him for that, just because she didn't agree with it. Just because her heart felt as if he had taken a sledgehammer to it and smashed it into a thousand little pieces.

'I think you'll understand if I don't show any interest in hearing about this *perfect bride* of yours,' she said. 'I don't think I'm quite modern enough to do that.'

Pushing back her chair, she got to her feet, aware that the mother of the toddler was still looking at them. 'We've said all there is to say, Murat. I don't think there's any point in prolonging this, do you?'

She walked out of the café without a backward glance but it seemed that he wasn't letting go of her that easily. Outside, he caught her by the arm and she whirled around, the soft rain on her face mingling with the tears she couldn't hold back any longer.

'What is it you want from me?' she demanded brokenly.

'You know the answer to that. I want you.'

'Well, you can't have me. Not in the way you mean. I won't be your mistress any more. I…can't. It's over, Murat, so leave me alone. Please. Promise me that much at least.'

There was a long silence, broken only by the caw-ing sound of distant seagulls. She thought his face looked almost grey now. That it matched the sky and the sea and her heart.

'I promise,' he said.

It was only when she heard the break in his voice that she realised her own heartache was mirrored in his eyes. And it came as something of a shock to realise that Murat was struggling to hold onto his own composure.

# CHAPTER TWELVE

MURAT PACED THROUGH the room, oblivious to the gleam of gold or subtle scent of sandalwood, or to the hawk-faced portrait of his great-great-grandfather, which glowered down from above the mighty oak desk. He was oblivious to everything except the cold and heavy feeling in his heart.

There was a tap on the door and he knew he could no longer ignore his advisor. For wasn't it the mark of a coward to hide from something he could not bear to face?

'Come!' he said, and the huge door opened to admit Bakri, the trusted emissary who had been with him since his friend Suleiman had left to make himself a fortune.

Carefully closing the door behind him, Bakri walked into the room and bowed deeply.

'Sire, I am pressed to remind you that your decision cannot be delayed for much longer. The delegation from Jabalahstan grows impatient for your decision.'

'It is not their place to *grow impatient*,' said Murat,

his barely restrained anger beginning to erupt at last. 'I have told them that I will give an answer once my deliberations are concluded and they are not concluded yet.'

'I understand that.' Bakri cleared his throat. 'And if I can be of any assistance in helping you to arrive at that decision, sire, then it will be both my honour and my duty.'

Duty. There it was again. That damnable word which haunted royal men from the moment they left the cradle. Murat gave a heavy sigh as he turned to look out of the windows overlooking the palace gardens. This room had been his father's—and his father's before that—all the way back along the Al Maisan line, from when the mighty palace had first been built. It was a place to which women were never admitted, and previously he would have considered such a restriction both right and fitting. For it was a place where wars had been plotted. Where kingdoms had been argued over before inevitable divisions were made. It was a very masculine room where once he would never have been able to envisage the softness of a woman. But now…

Now he found his mind playing tricks with him. He had started to imagine Cat standing there. Cat with her long dark hair tumbling down her back. Cat clad in the softly flowing robes of a Qurhahian Sultana.

He shook his head, but still he could not shake off the tantalising image. Just as he could not escape from her presence in every dream he'd had since returning from England. It seemed that the impossible had happened.

His heart ached.

He could not think straight.

And for the first time in his life, he was unsure what to do.

Just before he'd left, he had told her that he loved her, thinking that such an admission would be cathartic. That he could let out those strange feelings which had gripped his heart so intensely and then he would be free of them. But he was not free of them. On the contrary, he was bound by them as surely as if they were chains of iron. He missed her as much as he had done from the beginning and he wanted her even more.

He thought about the way he'd felt as his car had driven away from that little Welsh seaside town. How the tears had slid noiselessly down his cheeks, unseen by anyone else, but startling him, all the same. He had only ever cried once before and that had been when his mother had died. He had been brought up in a culture where strength was everything; where it was considered wrong for a man to ever show his feelings. And that had never been a problem before, because he'd never *had* real feelings for a woman before.

But suddenly, he was consumed by them.

He looked at the portrait above the desk, at the fierce expression of the ancient Sultan and those hard and glittering black eyes which marked out all the

Al Maisan men. He thought about what *his* life must have been like and then compared it to his own.

His mind went back to the things Cat had said to him, just before he'd left. Her breathless words and the appeal in her eyes had haunted him for days afterwards. He had tried very hard not to think about her, but that hadn't worked either. And suddenly he found himself wondering how he could have been so...*stupid*.

He turned to Bakri and his emissary tensed, as if he had seen something in his monarch's face which was momentous.

'I cannot marry the princess,' said Murat and his words sounded flat and hard as they echoed around that high-ceilinged room.

'But, sire—'

'Yes,' said Murat. 'I know what you're going to say, Bakri and that you will be justified. I realise that I cannot continue to behave like this. That it isn't fair to the women in question, nor is it fair to my people to keep refusing to marry, and to provide them with the heir which they long for. But I have a solution.'

Bakri narrowed his eyes. 'You do?'

'I do,' said Murat grimly. 'Get me Gabe Steel on the phone, will you?'

Catrin stared at the general manager as if she hadn't heard him properly. 'Could you...um...repeat that?' she questioned.

Stephen Le Saux nodded, and smiled. 'Of course. We're very pleased with you, Catrin. You've worked very hard and shown great promise since you've been here. You've proved that you can turn your hand to pretty much anything and we'd like you to fly down to the Cornish hotel in our group. The assistant general manager has been taken ill and we need a safe pair of hands to help them cope, until she's back on her feet. And it's been decided that you would be the perfect candidate.'

Catrin swallowed, guessing that praise was exactly what she needed at a time like this, though she couldn't deny her surprise. It was an honour to be asked, yes—but did she deserve it? She had been trying to work hard ever since Murat had gone back to Qurhah, but her heart hadn't really been in it. Maybe it was difficult for a heart to be enthusiastic about anything when it felt so empty. As if there were a hole in your chest where that heart used to be.

She'd gone about her work, thinking—hoping?— that Murat might telephone, even though she had told herself that she wouldn't pick up. But he hadn't. There had been nothing but a very loud silence from the Middle East, forcing her to face a truth she didn't want to face. It seemed that it really *was* over. And even though she knew they couldn't have carried on like that it didn't stop her from feeling as if her world had suddenly become muted. As if a dark curtain had descended and shrouded everything which was bright and good.

'You'll need your passport, for ID purposes,' Stephen Le Saux was saying. 'And you'll need to be ready in an hour. We'll be flying you down to Newquay this afternoon, if that's okay?'

'That soon?' questioned Catrin, standing up and smoothing her palms down over her uniform dress.

'Unless you have something keeping you here?'

She would have laughed, if laughing hadn't become such an alien concept. 'No, there's nothing keeping me here,' she said.

She went directly to her room. At least other areas of her life were looking good. Rachel was doing well at Uni and her mother was doing even better in Arizona. Even though all contact with the outside world had been banned for the first six weeks of treatment, Catrin had spoken to one of the counsellors at the clinic, who had sounded cautiously optimistic about her progress.

Hastily, she packed a bag and was ready and waiting when the hotel mini-bus arrived to take her to Cardiff airport, with Stephen himself at the wheel. But she started feeling confused when they got to the airport and he took her straight to a rather plush waiting room.

'Are you sure I'm in the right place?' she questioned as she looked around to see several smartly dressed people sipping from glasses of champagne.

'Of course you are,' he answered smoothly. 'And you'll be well looked after, I can assure you. Have a good trip.'

Catrin had only ever travelled by air with Murat, with his staff making all the arrangements, and in a way this seemed no different. Maybe that was what made her so compliant—allowing herself to be shown onto a plane which was much larger than she'd expected for a relatively short flight to Cornwall. And it wasn't until they were in the air—indeed, until they were crossing the English Channel that she started to realise that something was very wrong. For a start, she was the *only person on the plane* and the stunning redhead stewardess was treating her as if she were some kind of *royalty*.

Catrin summoned her over with a hand which had suddenly started trembling. 'Would you mind telling me where this plane is headed?'

The redhead smiled. 'Why, to Qurhah, of course.'

Catrin's mouth opened, closed, then opened again. 'But I'm supposed to be going to Cornwall.'

The redhead's smile grew wider. 'I don't think so,' she said gently. 'This is one of the Sultan's jets and you are the esteemed guest of the Sultan himself. You're flying to Simdahab, the capital of Qurhah.'

Catrin wanted to leap from her seat and say that she wasn't going anywhere, and certainly not to Qurhah to see a man she couldn't have. A man she was doing her level best to forget, who had now decided in some outrageously macho way to actually *kidnap* her. But she could hardly demand a parachute and throw herself out of the plane, could she? Especially when her knees were feeling so weak that she didn't think she'd be able to stand, let alone make a dash for it.

With an angry little sound, she sat back in the plush seat, shaking her head when the stewardess offered her a glass of lime juice. But the long flight meant that she couldn't keep refusing drinks, or food, even though she merely picked at the tempting morsels she was offered.

Her gaze kept steering to the window, though the skies were now in darkness. But where the flicker of the plane lights passed over the ground, she could see the stark desert sands which Murat had spoken of so many times. And as the plane began its descent she could do nothing to prevent the shiver which ran down her spine, hating her reaction because she understood exactly what had caused it. Because this was the land which had spawned him. The land which had made Murat the cold-eyed warrior who had broken her heart.

So why had he brought her here? Against her will and against her knowledge?

She supposed that she could refuse to leave her seat, cling on tightly and demand to be flown back to Wales. But there was no way she could behave like that and maintain any degree of dignity, and she told herself that maintaining her dignity was paramount. Yet it wasn't *just* that, was it? She was curious to know what had made Murat do something like this. He had promised to leave her alone and it seemed that he had broken his word—and it was that which surprised her more than anything.

A man called Bakri came onto the plane and introduced himself as Murat's aide. It was weird, because, although she'd sometimes spoken to him when he'd phoned Murat in London, Catrin had never imagined she would actually meet him. She had never thought that her world would collide with the Sultan's like this.

*And she still didn't know why it had.*

Bakri was extremely courteous, but he stone-walled all her indignant questions with the mantra: 'The Sultan will tell you everything you wish to know.'

Feeling slightly ridiculous in her jeans and T-shirt, Catrin walked down the aircraft steps to alight on Qurhahian soil and looked up into the starriest sky she had ever seen. She had removed her sweater on the plane but the fierce heat which hit her now was like being hurled into the centre of a furnace. She wondered where Murat was. Why he was not waiting at the bottom of the steps to meet her.

And then suddenly she heard a distant thunder, which gradually morphed into the unmistakable sound of approaching hooves. Her head jerked up to see a huge black stallion cantering towards her and Catrin's heart missed a beat.

The man on the horse's back could have been any man, with his anonymous flowing robes and a headdress billowing behind him. But it wasn't just any man. She would have recognised that powerful frame anywhere, even before the rider grew close enough for her to see his stern and hawk-like face.

'Murat,' she gasped. 'What the *hell* is going on?'

But he didn't answer, just leaned right over and caught hold of her before lifting her up onto the saddle. And Catrin was so shocked by the apparent ease of this action that she leaned back into him as he clamped his arm tightly around her waist, dug his thighs into the horse's flanks and set off.

It felt surreal. The airport buildings receded and tarmac roads soon gave way to sand as the horse entered the desert with a low whinny of delight.

Catrin's heart was pounding wildly, though she wasn't sure if that was from fear, or bewilderment, or the sheer excitement of being pressed up close to Murat's hard body, with his arm locked tightly around her. There were no signs, but he kept looking up at the stars as if he was seeking guidance from those celestial signposts which never changed.

She didn't know how long they galloped for, only that it felt like the most exhilarating journey of her life—but at some point she realised that a canopied dwelling had appeared in the distance and that Murat was heading towards it. And, minutes later, he brought the horse to a standstill in front of what looked like a very large tent.

But as he jumped down from the stallion and then raised his arms to lift her gently down onto the sand, Catrin realised that this was like no tent she'd ever seen.

Fretwork lamps stood in a glowing circle outside, casting intricate shadows onto the heavy canvas. The shadowed figure of a servant pulled back two lavishly embroidered flaps to reveal the lavish interior within.

'Come,' said Murat, adding something in Qurhahian, which caused the servant to melt into the darkness.

Still feeling shell-shocked, Catrin followed Murat into a lantern-lit room of unbelievable splendour. A long day-bed was covered by throws of gold and scarlet silk and heaped with a mishmash of silken cushions. On an engraved table stood a silver pot of what smelled like very strong coffee and beside it were two tiny silver cups. The air was scented with sandalwood though it was underpinned by something much richer and sweeter, something which might have been tuberose.

Catrin turned to see the low divan which stood at the far end of the tent and when she turned back again it was to find Murat's eyes on her, his expression intense and very watchful. She studied him right back, acknowledging that this was a Murat she had never seen before, looking as if he had stepped straight from the pages of an ancient fable. And she hated the leap her heart gave nearly as much as she hated the way that her eyes ran so greedily over his powerful frame.

He looked…unfamiliar. She had never seen him in his desert robes before and she thought how unfair it was that she had not been given a chance to prepare herself for the impact of that.

He was all dark and gleaming power. The pale gold of the flowing garments emphasised the much darker hue of his skin, and somehow managed to emphasise the hard body beneath. His hair was covered by a matching headdress, knotted with an in-

tricately woven circlet of black silk. And even that
was a turn-on. She thought how privileged she had
been to see the Sultan's hair in a past life. To have
run her fingers through it and kissed it.

Catrin's hand flew to her throat in horror.

*Privileged to see his hair?*

Had she been slipped some kind of drug while
she'd been on board the plane, which had wiped her
brain clear of any logic or reason? She glared at him.
Had he brought her here for his pleasure? To make
love to his erstwhile Welsh mistress, before inevitably casting her aside for the princess he would one
day marry?

'Why have you brought me here, Murat? What
the *hell* is going on?'

His gaze was steady; his eyes like chips of black
ice.

'I had to see you.'

She swallowed, telling herself not to fall for it.
She couldn't afford to fall for it. 'Even if you did,'
she said, sucking in a deep breath and trying to slow
down the rapid thunder of her heart, 'couldn't you
have just gone about it using normal channels? Ever
thought of sending an email or even phoning?'

'And would you have answered?' he demanded.
'Would you have been prepared to come here, if I
had asked you to? If I told you that the need to see
you felt as imperative to me as breathing itself, would
you have listened to me?'

There was no doubting the deeply poetic nature
of his words, and no doubting that it made her heart

race even more to hear them. And they certainly *sounded* sincere. But Catrin kept her face set in a mulish expression, instinct warning her to protect herself behind the steely armour of anger. 'I don't appreciate being bundled onto an aircraft and flown halfway around the world,' she spat out, 'just to satisfy some stupid *whim* of yours. How on earth did you manage to get my boss to cooperate?'

'I asked him.'

'Or bribed him, more likely.'

'There was no need to resort to such methods. Though I can't deny that I would have employed them if necessary,' he said, with a smile obviously designed to make her melt. 'In fact, he seemed rather captivated by the love-story aspect of my request.'

'But there *is* no love story!' She walked over to the other side of the tent, because his proximity was making it difficult for her to breathe. 'Your "love" is currently on ice—just waiting for Princess Lucky to waltz in and melt it.'

For a moment he said nothing, just let his gaze travel over her very slowly as if he'd never really seen her properly before.

'Oh, Cat,' he said softly. 'You are magnificent.'

'No, Murat, *you're* the one who's supposed to be magnificent, not me. And…' Some of her bravado was leaving her now. Suddenly she was feeling very alone—and scared. Scared of the way he could make her feel and scared of how much more he could hurt her. And she couldn't afford to let him hurt her, not any more. Because she was strong Cat, not weak Cat.

She was Cat who didn't cry and yet these stupid tears were pricking away at the backs of her eyes. 'It's a cheap trick to bring me out here into the middle of nowhere, where I'm effectively at your mercy.'

He said nothing, just walked across the room and took her hand, bringing her fingertips to his mouth and leaving them there, so that when he spoke she could feel the warmth of his breath against her skin. And Catrin was appalled to discover that she wasn't pulling away. That she was just standing there and *letting* him touch her.

'And is it a cheap trick to ask you to be my bride, Cat?' he questioned. 'To be my Sultana and help me rule over the people of Qurhah for as long as we both shall live?'

Snatching her hand away, she moved away from him again—as if they were both participants in some old-fashioned dance. 'Do you get some kind of kick out of tormenting me?' she gritted. 'When we both know that I *can't* be your bride.'

'Oh, but you can,' he argued and he was coming towards her once again. Like some persistent wave you saw at the edge of the ocean, he just kept on coming. 'Sweet *habibti* of mine—you can. I wouldn't dream of asking you something as important as this, unless it was possible.'

His shadow loomed over her and she stared up into those night-dark eyes, searching for some sign that he was tricking her. Because she couldn't risk believing him. She couldn't risk having all her hopes raised heavenwards and then smashed down again.

'How is it possible?' She crossed her arms over her breasts. 'How?'

'I spoke to my brother-in-law, Gabe, who is one of the few men I trust. He knew of my dilemma. That I loved you but that my hands were tied. Because how could the Sultan possibly break the law of his own land? I told him about the things you'd said. Things which I'd previously refused to think about, only now I had a reason to think about them very seriously. About modern countries needing to move with the times. And Gabe agreed. He said that it was archaic and unrealistic to expect a law which had been written centuries ago to apply to a modern sultan in a modern age.

'So I had my attorney general redraft the constitution,' he continued. 'It just took it a little time before it all became official. It was rubber-stamped yesterday. And that's why I have brought you here, Cat. To tell you that I have had the law changed in order to marry you. But also to tell you something else, other than the fact I love you very much.' He sucked in a deep breath. 'And that is you have made me more of a man than I thought it was possible to be. You have made me *feel* things, my beauty. Things that sometimes make me feel almost scared but which at other times fill me with the kind of joy I didn't believe existed. Most of all, they make me feel *alive*.'

Her chest felt tight and she could hardly breathe, let alone speak, but that was okay because it seemed that Murat had not yet finished.

'Shall I tell you what my life feels like without

you?' he questioned. 'It's cold and there's no light any more, as if somebody has covered up the sun. I feel as if part of me is missing—and it's the best part. I am empty without you, Cat, and I can't imagine a future if you're not a part of it. Which is why I am asking you to forgive me for some of my more outrageous behaviour of the past, and to be my wife and let me spend the rest of my life loving you as you should be loved.'

Catrin felt her heart flare as if somebody had just warmed it with a naked flame. She thought about the kindness he'd shown to her mother and the gentleness with which he had treated her when she'd been sick. She saw the look of love in his eyes and it would have been so easy to have capitulated. To have fallen eagerly into his arms and told him that she would marry him, because he was the only man she would ever love.

'I can't,' she said.

At this he rocked back on his heels, black brows knitting together in disbelief as he stared at her and now Catrin could see a touch of his customary arrogance.

'What do you mean, you can't? You love me, don't you, Cat? You may tell me that you don't, but your eyes can't hide the fact.'

'Yes, I love you,' she said. 'But I can't live the kind of life you're offering me.'

'You mean that you don't want to live here? That you cannot bear the thought of being Sultana and bringing up our children in a desert palace?'

The *our children* bit nearly made her buckle, but Catrin knew she had to be strong.

'I can't bear the thought of you having a harem,' she said quietly. 'Or keeping mistresses, as you once told me that your father had done.'

'Mistresses?' he roared. 'Do you imagine that there is any woman I could bear to have near to me, unless she was you? Don't you know how completely you have captured my heart and my body and my soul and made them all your own, my darling one?'

'Murat—'

'I love you, Catrin Thomas,' he whispered. 'Now, for ever and always. Exclusively. Let me tell you that I want you to be my wife and I will not rest until you have consented.'

She was done then. She couldn't keep fighting her heart's desire, not when she wanted and needed him nearly as much as breath itself.

'Oh, Murat,' she said. 'My darling Murat.'

There were tears as she went into his arms but he kissed them all away until there were no tears left. And after a long while, he extinguished all the lamps and led her over to the low divan and it was there, on that warm night in the middle of the desert, that they came together, vowing to love and to cherish each other for the rest of their days.

# EPILOGUE

'READY?'

'As I'll ever be.' Catrin looked up into Murat's eyes as he gave her hand a squeeze.

'Scared?' he questioned.

She looped her arms around his neck, taking care not to crease the exquisite silk of her suit jacket. 'With you by my side? Never in a million years. A bit nervous, yes, but that's perfectly normal.'

He ran his thumb along the edge of her jaw. 'I guess you've already been through quite a lot,' he said. 'It's been an action-packed year.'

He could say that again.

Their engagement had caused predictable excitement in the international press. A humble girl from the Welsh valleys marrying one of the world's richest royals was always going to be a big story in the tabloids—but it had also spawned many thoughtful pieces in the broadsheets. Much had been made about the fact that Qurhah seemed to be embracing the modern world by admitting that ancient laws could and would be changed. Privately, Catrin thought they'd rather overplayed the Cinderella aspect of the story and—as Rachel had pointed out rather indignantly—the Sultana-to-be only had *one* sister, and she wasn't in the least bit ugly!

Then some enterprising journalist had ferreted out an old photo of her mother in an inebriated state, dancing on a table in a pub and doing something regrettable with a feather boa. But Murat had told her flatly that he didn't care. Her mother was sober now and perhaps the picture might serve to remind her of how much better her life was today.

Then he had surprised much of the desert community by announcing that many of the ancient laws of his land were to be reassessed, in order to keep pace with the modern world.

A very grand Qurhahian wedding had followed the engagement. It had taken place in the beautiful royal palace in Simdahab and was attended by Sheikhs and Sultans; Prime Ministers and Kings, as well as various movers and shakers, and even a sprinkling of Hollywood. But Rachel was there, and several of the people Catrin had worked with in the hotel industry, including Stephen Le Saux, who was heard boasting that he had played matchmaker to the unlikely couple.

Two of Murat's oldest friends were there. Alekto Sarantos and Niccolo Da Conti were considered easily to be the best-looking guests in attendance, though the racing driver Luis Martinez had been forced to decline his invitation and there were all kinds of dark rumours swirling around as to why.

And the mother of the bride shone—looking about twenty years younger and giggling at something Murat's uncle was saying as he monopolised her during the glitzy reception afterwards. Ursula Thomas's recovery had given Catrin and Rachel so much joy. She had returned from the Arizona clinic looking the picture of health and happiness. She had started training as a counsellor herself and there was talk that she might open up her own clinic in the beautiful mountains of Wales, with her new son-in-law's assistance.

Murat's sister Leila was there, along with her husband, Gabe, who had been so instrumental in bringing together all the different parties necessary to change Qurhahian law. As he'd said, it was in his interests to do so, since his own son was half-Qurhahian.

And Catrin had instantly fallen in love with her nephew, Hafez. Her *nephew*! Her family seemed to have multiplied overnight…and who knew where it would all end? A couple of days before the wedding she had been cuddling Hafez and had glanced up to find Murat looking at her with a wry expression on his face. And she had looked at him and smiled and he had smiled back and, in that moment, the world had seemed as perfect as it was possible to be.

Sara was there too, with her husband Suleiman. And if Catrin had harboured any latent fears that Murat still hankered after the royal princess who had once been betrothed to him they were soon dispelled. Sara was so obviously deliriously happy with her oil-magnate husband, Suleiman, that their joy was infectious. And Catrin knew deep in her heart that Murat didn't really *see* any other woman but her.

Today was her first official engagement as the new Sultana, even though they had been married just over a year. But Catrin had thrown herself into preparation for her new role, not wanting to take on anything until she could do it justice. She didn't want to let the people of Qurhah down. She wanted to be the best Sultana she possibly could.

She loved Qurhah and had studied the history of her adopted homeland. She had also been diligent in learning the language—at which she had excelled. Apparently, having Welsh as a first language had helped her linguistic skills though, as Murat always said, she was a fast learner.

Today, she was opening a new wing in her name at the children's hospital, where Murat had once had his appendix removed. And after having afternoon tea with some of the young patients, the two of them were travelling for a short break at his summer palace.

She loved it there. It was there that they came as close to freedom as a monarch and his wife ever could. It was where he had taught her to ride and they took every opportunity they could to gallop some of his prized Akhal-Teke horses across the desert plains.

The landscape was magnificent—stark and stunning. Catrin thought that there was little to surpass

the magnificence of the sun setting over the famous
Mekathasinian Sands.

Only her husband managed to do that.

She touched her lips to his and met the smile in
his eyes.

Oh, yes.

It was easy to see why they called him Murat the
Magnificent.

\* \* \* \* \*

## #3233 SHEIKH'S SCANDAL
*The Chatsfield*
### by Lucy Monroe
The world's media is buzzing as brooding Sheikh Sayed and his harem take up residence at the exclusive Chatsfield Hotel...but an even bigger scandal threatens to break when a stolen night with chambermaid Liyah Amari results in an unexpected complication....

## #3234 THE ONLY WOMAN TO DEFY HIM
### by Carol Marinelli
Personal assistant Alina Ritchi finds her defiance ignited under the powerful gaze of legendary playboy Demyan Zukov. But when every shared touch sizzles, how long can Alina keep saying 'no' when her body wants to scream 'yes'?

## #3235 GAMBLING WITH THE CROWN
*Heirs to the Throne of Kyr*
### by Lynn Raye Harris
When Sheikh Kadir al Hassan promotes long-suffering assistant Emily Bryant to royal bride, he's convinced she'll be deemed so unsuitable he'll successfully avoid the crown. But one kiss forces Kadir to make the ultimate choice: his desert duty, or Emily!

## #3236 ONE NIGHT TO RISK IT ALL
### by Maisey Yates
Dutiful Rachel Holt has never put a foot wrong...until she reaches for one electrifying night with notorious Greek tycoon Alexios Christofides. But *this* one night has great consequences for them both, especially when Rachel realizes Alex's true identity!

HPCNM0414RA

## #3237 SECRETS OF A RUTHLESS TYCOON
### by Cathy Williams

There's one thing Leo Spencer's luxurious lifestyle can't give him—the truth about his past. His search for answers leads him to Brianna Sullivan, hidden in the Irish countryside, where she soon proves to be a distraction he never anticipated....

## #3238 THE FORBIDDEN TOUCH OF SANGUARDO
### by Julia James

Self-made millionaire Rafael Sanguardo *always* gets what he wants...and he wants Celeste Philips. Celeste knows she shouldn't fall for Rafael's practiced charm, yet the more her head tells her to walk away...the more she craves his forbidden touch!

## #3239 A CLASH WITH CANNAVARO
### by Elizabeth Power

Italian billionaire Emiliano Cannavaro is determined to regain custody of his orphaned nephew from Lauren Westwood—a woman he believes is after only one thing. But innocent Lauren won't give up without a fight—and it promises to be explosive!

## #3240 THE TRUTH ABOUT DE CAMPO
### by Jennifer Hayward

Matteo de Campo wants to secure a multi-million dollar deal with Quinn's family's company—which means she mustn't fall for his enticing appeal! But when Quinn glimpses his inner demons, she's determined to discover just *who* the real Matteo is....

---

# REQUEST YOUR FREE BOOKS!

HARLEQUIN *Presents*

PASSION GUARANTEED SEDUCTION

## 2 FREE NOVELS PLUS
# 2 FREE GIFTS!

SPECIAL EXCERPT FROM

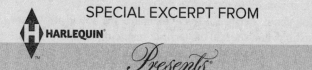

HARLEQUIN

*Presents*

*Harlequin Presents welcomes you to the world of
The Chatsfield—synonymous with style, spectacle...
and scandal! Read on for an exclusive extract from
Lucy Monroe's stunning story SHEIKH'S SCANDAL.
The first in an exciting new eight-book series:*
THE CHATSFIELD.

\* \* \*

THE guest elevators at The Chatsfield hotel in London were spacious by any definition, but the confined area *felt* small to Aaliyah Amari.

"You're not very Western in your outlook," she said, trying to ignore the unfamiliar desires and emotions roiling through her.

"I am the heart of Zeena Sahra—should my people and their ways not be the center of mine?"

She didn't like how much his answer touched her. To cover her reaction she waved her hand between the two of them and said, "This isn't the way of Zeena Sahra."

"You are so sure?" he asked.

"Yes."

He laughed, the honest sound of genuine amusement more compelling than even the uninterrupted regard of the extremely handsome man. "You are not like other women."

"You're the emir."

"You are saying other women are awed by me."

She gave him a wry look and said drily, "You're not conceited at all, are you?"

"Is it conceit to recognize the truth?"

She shook her head. Even arrogant, she found this man irresistible, and she had the terrible suspicion he knew it, too.

Unsure how she'd got there, she felt the wall of the elevator at her back. Sayed's body was so close his outer robes brushed her. Her breath came out on a shocked gasp.

He brushed her lower lip with his fingertip. "Your mouth is luscious."

"This is a bad idea."

"Is it?" he asked, his head dipping toward hers.

"Yes. I'm not part of the amenities."

"I know." His tone rang with sincerity.

"I don't do elevator romps," she clarified, just in case he didn't get it.

Something flared in his dark gaze and Sayed stepped back, shaking his head. "I apologize, Miss Amari. I do not know what came over me."

"I'm sure you're used to women falling all over you," she offered by way of an explanation.

He frowned. "Is that meant to be a sop to my ego or a slam against it?"

"Neither?"

He shook his head again, as if trying to clear it.

She wondered if it worked. She would be grateful for a technique that brought back her own usual way of thinking, unobscured by this unwelcome and unfamiliar desire.

\* \* \*

*Step into the gilded world of* THE CHATSFIELD!
*Where secrets and scandal lurk behind every door…*

*Reserve your room in May 2014!*

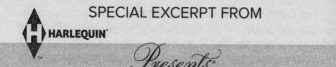
*Carol Marinelli brings you another spectacular book, full of passion, excitement and secrets! Read on for an extract from THE ONLY WOMAN TO DEFY HIM...*

\* \* \*

"COME on," Demyan Zukov rasped harshly. "I'll take you home."

He saw the flare of disappointment in Alina Ritchi's eyes.

Her body was warm, and Demyan stared at her all flushed and aroused, and was tempted to put his scruples on ice.

"We could go back...." Alina couldn't believe she'd just said that, but she had, and she meant every word.

"Alina," Demyan cut in bluntly. "I'm not going to be here for long."

"I know that," she intoned softly.

"I will be leaving Australia soon, and I have no intention of ever coming back," Demyan bit out harshly.

"I get that," Alina murmured.

"Alina, I'm not someone that you should be cutting your teeth on." He saw her blush, but he was simply telling her the truth. He was bad, he had no soul and he never looked back. "You need to have your molars," Demyan teased, because if he didn't carry on speaking he would kiss her again. "You need to have had your wisdom teeth out and your invisible braces long since gone before you even think of getting involved with a guy like me."

He drove her home, and Demyan could feel the disappointment oozing from her as they turned onto her street. "Eight o'clock Monday," Demyan said, and gave her a thin smile when he knew that she wanted a kiss. He tried to ignore the tears glittering in her eyes. "Back to business, Alina…" He caught her wrist, and to make things a little better, he lied. "I don't get involved with people I work with."

"Sure."

Alina knew he was lying.

Demyan could be very blunt at times. But what he didn't know was that he should have been just a little bit blunter. Had he simply said, *I don't do virgins,* Alina might better have understood.

As it was, she walked into her house, barricaded herself in her bedroom and then promptly burst into tears, having decided that it wasn't that they would be working together that was the problem.

Demyan simply didn't want her.

\* \* \*

*Demyan Zukov's never known a woman quite like Alina Ritchi. How will the notorious playboy handle his new assistant, who threatens to test his will?*

*Find out in May 2014!*

HPEXP0414-2-1

*Revenge and seduction intertwine…*

Maisey Yates's latest story is packed full of revenge, seduction and so much more.

### *The* ultimate *seduction!*

Greek tycoon Alexios Christofides is notorious for getting exactly what he wants. He's determined to wrench the Holt empire away from his enemy, and if that means seducing the man's stunning fiancée, innocent but oh-so-sweet Rachel Holt, then all the better!

# ONE NIGHT TO RISK IT ALL
## by
# *Maisey Yates*

### Available May 2014
### wherever books are sold!

HP13242